The Treasure of Gran Quivira

Copyright © 2007 Clyde Casey

ISBN-13 978-1-60145-151-4
ISBN-10 1-60145-151-2

All rights reserved. No part of this publication may be reproduced, stored in a retrieval system, or transmitted in any form or by any means, electronic, mechanical, recording or otherwise, without the prior written permission of the author.

Printed in the United States of America.

The characters and events in this book are fictitious. Any similarity to real persons, living or dead, is coincidental and not intended by the author.

Booklocker.com, Inc.
2007

The Treasure of Gran Quivira

Clyde Casey

Dedication

To my wife of over 50 years, without whom my life would have no meaning. Millie is my companion, my partner, and always my love.

Acknowledgements

Special thanks to: Leslie Andrews, Terry Casey, Edie Hughes, Eric, Jones, Darlene Jones, Carla Palmer, Mary Roby, Rosella Rodrigues, La Nelle Witt, for making this book publishable.

PROLOGUE

The years from 1610 to 1680 are known as the "Great Missionary Era" in New Mexico's fascinating history. Some 250 Spanish friars of the Franciscan order worked among the Pueblos during these decades and the Crown spent millions of dollars on salaries, supplies, and construction of churches.

During those years, the Franciscan padres launched an assault upon the very foundations of the Pueblo Indian religious structure. Unable to discredit their holy men, the friars used flogging and hanging in an effort to root out and destroy their "heathen practices," in particular the ceremonies conducted in kivas and at masked dances. Backed by Spanish soldiers, they raided the sacred chambers and defiled the Indian altars and murals. Gathering masks, prayer plumes, fetishes, and other holy paraphernalia, they burned them in the plazas.

After years of harsh treatment, the Indians banded together and in 1680 the Spaniards and their friars were driven from New Mexico.

One such account of their expulsion concerns three friars at Gran Quivira. Seventy-five yards downhill from the towering sandstone walls of the church, the three Long Coats crouched behind a clump of pinon trees. They listened to the screams of dying men and the yells of the Indians as they shielded themselves against the dry, bitter cold. The wind seemed to roar and howl around them as they finalized their escape plan. The Franciscans had built churches and done their best to bring Christianity to these heathens, but the Indians still rebelled. Why would they want to turn from God's infinite mercy and return to their abominable practices, profaning the sanctuary, destroying sacred images and ornaments, and were now prepared to commit other atrocities too heinous to contemplate?

In their hearts the Long Coats knew the Indians would one day regain their senses and welcome back Christianity. In the meantime, the Long Coats knew they had concealed their treasure well. Now was the time to leave this barren land and head south to Mexico.

CHAPTER 1
Crownpoint New Mexico

Six foot, handsome, gallery owner Miguel Jaramillo is a study in brown. From his well-groomed almost black hair, to his buff suede Western jacket to his Tony Lama boots, he looks like a model from a New Mexico Fashion Magazine. The clear blue of turquoise in the masculine Navajo jewelry of his matching bolo tie, watch band, ring, and belt buckle pop against the neutral pallet. He's dressed for work.

Standing quietly against one wall Miguel observes the flurried pre-auction activity of a milling crowd of people clustering around long tables stacked high with Navajo weavings. Meanwhile dozens of prospective bidders are pawing weavings, jotting down notes of the tag numbers on scraps of paper, notebooks, and assorted electronic devices.

Arriving early, he has already selected the weavings that he plans to bid on. Now he amuses himself by observing how the prospective buyers attempt to hide their excitement when they find a piece they intend to purchase.

This large, public auction is held each month in gymnasium of the Crownpoint High School, northwest of Albuquerque, New Mexico. Today it hosts more than 200 dealers plus a few tourists who have dropped in hoping to find a bargain. Some will, some will only think they have.

Miguel considers his day a success so far. At the chili supper served before the auction started, an auctioneer, whom he knew by reputation and personal experience, gave him a lead on a large, not yet advertised, estate sale with more than 175 Navajo rugs and blankets. Many of them were said to be at least 100 years old. Since he is always ready to pay cash, he's found some estate heirs are willing to accept his pre-auction offers, and at times has been able to buy a number of key pieces before the auctions started. It's a practice allowing the sellers to avoid taxes and is fairly common in large estate sales. Miguel knows a trader's success is based on his ability to find quality work for resale and he's excited to have a chance to bid on a collection of such magnitude.

A little later, taking his seat in the third row, he watches as the other bidders whisper to each other comparing notes. Several times he notices an elderly homeless looking gentleman, leaning against the wall, who seems to be observing him too closely. Preferring to maintain a low profile, he is uneasy with this kind of attention. Still it's probably nothing. Auctions always make him tense. Looking at the number of tourists, he realizes it will be a long evening.

"Sold to number eighty-seven." The auctioneer's words ring out as his gavel hits the block for the last time. It's 11:39 p.m. Freeing himself from the uncomfortable metal folding chair, Miguel stands up, stretches, and strolls toward the exit. He nods to several acquaintances, weavers, dealers, and collectors as he keeps moving.

Tonight's bidding was heated at times. The two auctioneers were entertaining, and on several occasions provoked a few laughs. Now, near the front, apparently oblivious to the commotion of 200 people leaving the gym, three young Navajo boys are making their own commotion, clanging the empty chairs while folding and stacking them on wooden pallets.

Miguel wearily wades through bidders clustering in small groups, jamming the narrow aisle. Working his way toward the back exit, he passes a large group of Navajo women dressed in their traditional velvet blouses, long skirts and heavy turquoise jewelry. Many of them are the weavers of the just auctioned rugs. Their imposing features are quiet, and it's difficult to determine if they are pleased with the prices their work has brought. In the days before the Crownpoint Rug Weavers Association Auctions was established, He and his father dealt with a number of these women individually, and came to recognize the apparent calmness of Navajo women often belies their inner glee, displeasure or even turmoil.

The weavings offered tonight are referred to as 'honest rugs,' not always prizewinners or collector items, but rugs guaranteed to have been woven in the old way. However, a few of these jewels were woven by expert weavers who raised the sheep, then sheared, cleaned, carded, and spun the wool. And as usual, these garnered the most attention and stole the show.

Miguel's special interest is in older weavings, but a certain number of his customers, primarily interior decorators, are always in the market for good contemporary pieces. Two of Miguel's clients had made special requests for room size contemporary pieces, but tonight, he chose not to purchase any.

The auction opened with a beautiful, eight-by twelve rug, representing a year's work from Clara Lapahie, a well-known Granada area weaver. Miguel did his best to obtain the black/red beauty, but stopped bidding when it hit $4,450.00. It was a fine example of Clara's work, but the bid was too high for resale. As for the other rugs, with a few exceptions, they were of excellent quality. However, they simply but did not represent the superior workmanship Miguel's expert eye demanded. Other than the large Granada he bid on, only six exceptional weavings were offered. Astute collectors purchased these at prices that were too close to retail.

Miguel is greeted just outside the door by a slightly stooped, white-haired Navajo elder who pokes him in the shoulder, in a friendly manner.

"*Senõr* Jaramillo," the elder says with a twinkle in his eye, "my wife wants to show you something."

With a jerk of his head, he motions for Miguel to follow him. Miguel knows his wife, Desbah Begay is one of the great Navajo weavers, and follows the old Indian to the back of the parking lot where an elderly Navajo woman, sits in the back of a dilapidated red pickup. Miguel lifts her from the bed of the pickup, and Desbah smells of wood smoke, lard from last night's fry bread, sheep dung, and a day's travel in a pickup truck. Her scent clinging tightly to him. To Miguel, these are the familiar odors of his youth and not the least offensive.

Her voice wavering, she says. "Long time no see, Miguel, you want to look at a big one?"

"Of course," Miguel replies. "You look good."

"Not good. My hands are old. Fingers like twigs. Hard to weave after almost seventy years."

The old woman couldn't weigh more than a hundred pounds. Her rounded back and shoulders tell of her many years at a vertical loom, her fingers are gnarled from pulling and tugging at the wool threads.

"I'm sorry to hear you are not well." Miguel says, setting her on the ground. "How's your daughter doing?"

"She's okay, but not weaving. She says its too much work. Help me." she demands, pointing to a rug.

Miguel helps her tug a large, rolled up rug from the bed of the old pickup, a rug still warm from the more than 105-degree temperature of a typical late July day in central New Mexico. After making sure the hot asphalt is not weeping tar and aided by her husband and Miguel, Desbah spreads out the weaving on the parking lot under a nearby light pole. Beautifully woven, it measures fourteen feet in length by eight feet in width and features the Klagetoh's familiar, dramatic, red-black-gray-white design of delicately woven terraces, a complex pattern of the sort instantly recognizable by experts. Miguel takes a flashlight from his briefcase and studies it closely, spotting some signs of wear. However, the rug itself is in excellent condition with a glossy sheen on the aged wool threads. Even under the sodium lighting of the parking lot, the old weaving is impressive.

Miguel notices a small round brass tag stamped with the letters URXR and the number 109 riveted to one corner. He's handled a few old rugs with similar tags and recognizes the tag as one used by the United Indian Trading Association, (U.I.T.A.). The U.I.T.A., no longer active, was a very early association of trading post owners, started in the late 1930's. The Association used these brass tags to identify their goods. The rug, at least fifty years old, had probably been in and out of pawn at a trading post near Grants, New Mexico.

"Desbah, is this your work?" He asks.

"Do you remember my older sister Cora?"

"Yes I do. Did she weave this?"

"Yes, a long time ago. I'm selling it for her. She's not well. Too many cigarettes. What will you give?"

Miguel continues to look it over very carefully. With a good professional cleaning, it will probably bring somewhere in the range of seven thousand dollars. He's also aware he may have to display it in his gallery for two or three years before he finds an astute collector who will truly appreciate a rug of this type. He's also sure Desbah doesn't realize its true value. But knowing how the old woman likes to haggle, he's prepared.

"Okay," he says getting to his feet. "I'll give you nine hundred." Without saying a word, Desbah starts to roll up the rug.

"What does your sister want for it then?" Miguel asks. "It's nice, but it's not new."

"I told her you would give her more," Desbah replies quietly. Taking another look at the weaving, Miguel asks, "How much more?"

"Much." She pauses, her leathered face caught in a scowl. "The highest I can go is eighteen hundred. Cash," Miguel announces after a long pause, during which Desbah continues to look concerned.

"Desbah it's a very old rug."

It's a paltry offer, but he feels sure she will take it. Desbah glances at her husband and then nods. "Okay," she says, "where's the money?"

Pulling out his billfold, Miguel counts out the agreed amount. Desbah meticulously inspects each bill again. "Thank you, Miguel," she says. "You're a good man."

Thanking the old woman, he asks her to give Cora his best. The couple climb back into their decrepit old pickup and drive off, leaving Miguel to amble toward his van, his latest acquisition slung over his shoulder.

In the shadows near the entrance, the strange little, homeless man heaves a sigh of relief as he watches Miguel Jaramillo leaving. The sweltering July day has taken its toll on Armando Peralta. The semi-retired private investigator considers this stakeout, deep in the Navajo Nation, to be a real drag. But a job is a job, even though in this case, there's little more to do than observe Miguel Jaramillo from a safe distance. Armando blends in with the crowd and although he's dressed like a homeless person, no one pays any attention to him. After years of surveillance the old private investigator has learned to observe without being observed.

A sharp pain in his lower back reminds him it's time to take another pill. At least the end of this tedious job is in sight. Scratching a few lines in a small notepad, he turns and limps toward his black Ford sedan, his bent shadow is distorted in the deep dent in the left rear quarter panel. Once behind the wheel, he rolls down all the windows to vent the oven-like interior. He has a few moments before he has to leave. After punching numbers into his cell phone, he begins his report.

***

Miguel uses the long trip back to Albuquerque to contemplate his expanding business activities.

With two busy galleries to oversee, he rarely finds a minute for himself, which is the reason he looks forward to going on buying trips like this one.

Behind the wheel, listening to mariachi music, he does some of his best planning. Driving along the back road of the reservation, he enjoys the cloudless night sky filled with millions of stars. During the day this dusty, high desert is barren except for an occasional grove of pinion pine or juniper and its blowing sands often make it inhospitable. But this night is crystal clear and a full moon lights up the countryside. Coming to a stretch of pavement roughened in preparation for a new asphalt seal coat, he drives more slowly. The roaring noise caused by the scuffed surface almost drowns out the mariachi music. On several occasions, Miguel's attention is drawn to vague shapes along the side of the road, as the eerily glowing eyes of a skunk or red fox pierce the darkness.

Louis Aragon Jaramillo, Miguel's father, was a successful, respected dealer of Navajo crafts until his untimely fatal heart attack. The son of Jose and Amalia who immigrated to the United States from Mexico in the early 30's, and became citizens in 1951. Louis served in Viet Nam, returning to New Mexico after the conflict, determined to look at beautiful things for the rest of his life. Already married to the loveliest lady he had ever known, Louis went to work in his wife's father's small import business in Albuquerque's Old Town. With Louis's help, the business thrived. Then after his father-in law's untimely death, Louis moved the business to a larger location and transformed it into his first art gallery.

Louis proved to be a tough trader and excellent businessman. When Miguel joined his father in the business, a delighted Louis often bragged to everyone about his son, who inherited his deep resonant voice, was an excellent listener, and an even better salesman. However, after Louis's death, some said that Miguel carried salesmanship too far and took advantage of Native Americans, even though he justified the low prices he paid for their efforts by arguing that his galleries were faced with ever increasing tough competition.

Miguel is still single at thirty-three, never having found any woman to share his love of art and passion for the history of the West. He has managed to visit most of New Mexico's historical sites on his many buying trips. It's during these travels he's developed a deep love for the Land of Enchantment. The more he travels through its colorful Spanish villages and adobe pueblos, the more he becomes intrigued with its history and his own heritage.

Miguel, like his father, also spent some time in the U.S. Army. After serving in the First Gulf war, he studied to become a chef.

It was only when his father became ill that Miguel dropped out of culinary school and went to work with him. Two difficult years later, after his father passed away, he became the sole owner/operator of his father's two art galleries in Albuquerque and Santa Fe. Here his clients include tourists, interior decorators, and many of the wealthy Hollywood celebrities who call Santa Fe their second home.

The oldest Jaramillo gallery is still located on its original site in the square of the Old Town Plaza of Albuquerque, a Mecca for the thousands of tourists who visited every year. His second prime location is in Santa Fe, off Galisteo Street. Now, with the annual Santa Fe Indian Art Market only a few weeks away, Miguel considers the possibility that he may not have selected the right inventory for the thousands of buyers who will be in town for the annual celebration of Indian Arts and Crafts. The celebration is nicknamed the "Million Dollar Baby." His gallery is stocked with the finest Western art, Indian pottery, and jewelry and always features a large selection of traditional Navajo weavings. In past years, his gallery has consistently been fortunate enough to capture a significant percentage of the Navajo rug sales generated by this colorful two-week gala.

Miguel realizes he must enhance his image if he is to continue to be successful, because the market is always changing. Although his new web site registers a number of hits, sales on line are not yet impressive. The younger clients who frequent his galleries are more interested in the contemporary work of R.C. Gorman's paintings of native women with big feet, than they are in any of the traditional artists like Sharpe, with his beautiful poetic renditions of Native Americans. Traffic is up in both galleries, but sales this year to date are down. As a consequence this year's Santa Fe Indian Art Market is particularly important.

Miguel traveled to Las Vegas, Nevada several times this past summer. He is considering opening a third gallery there. But first, he wants to see how well his inventory selections sell before making a final commitment to expansion. Obtaining sellable inventory has been difficult and obtaining enough of the right kind of inventory for a third gallery could be a real problem. The art market is tricky, however he feels that he knows it as well as anyone in the business.

He continues his journey with the music turned down low and looses himself in the serene beauty of the night, ignoring the car following him closely, just as he ignores the manila envelope Armando placed in clear view on the rear seat of his minivan.

CHAPTER 2
Albuquerque New Mexico

The early morning Albuquerque air is fresh and crisp as Doctor Armida Valentina Valenzuela turns onto the Rio Grande Bosque trail. Starting to run slowly, she gradually lengthens her strides as her lean body warms and her muscles relax. By the time she approaches a burned area of the trail she is running easily. She glances to her left, and feels her nostrils tingle from traces of the lingering odors of acrid smoke. Recent acts of arson have all but destroyed this section, one of her favorite areas of the joggers' trail. She notes the fire's black residue and can't help but be a little wistful, realizing that many years will be required to return the area to its lush, green beauty. Picking up her pace, she approaches a pristine area untouched by fire and realizes someone is closing in fast behind her. Armida has ran here for years and is a little uneasy but not alarmed. She's aware that multiple rape attacks are known to have occurred near here, and is relieved when she recognizes the young man. Her competitive nature kicks in as he draws near, and she effortlessly speeds away from him.

A short time later, Armida reaches the public parking lot that was her starting point, and with a towel wrapped around her neck, stretches her long legs beside her BMW. Her sweaty T-shirt clinging to her braless breasts. As the young man, passes by her, he stammers a clumsy "Good morning Professor." As he climbs into an old style Volkswagen and speeds away, Armida stares after him curiously. She's accustomed to having men look at her but wonders briefly why he seemed so awkward, and then forgetting the encounter, finishes her stretching routine. Refreshed by her run and safe inside her BMW, she drives back to her condo in time to shower, change, and grab a bite before she leaves for work.

Armida sits at her desk, contemplating her schedule. Her leave of absence, financed by a fellowship grant from the National Endowment for the Humanities Travels to Collection programs, is finished and today is her first full day back at the University of New Mexico's Taylor Museum. She's grateful the Museum's directors have allowed her the necessary travel time to gather materials for her manuscript. Her current study is based upon thousands of pounds of Navajo weavings, and the directors are pleased with the result of her efforts, her second book on Navajo weaving is scheduled for publication in the spring. After visiting fifteen other museums, she has learned to appreciate the true depth of the Taylor's vast collections. Using her Palm Pilot, she sketches out a tentative schedule for completing the cataloging of the museum's extensive collection of American Indian artifacts. Armida's area of expertise, Native American Indians of the Southwest, flourishes here, and she's anxious to get back to her regular duties.

She's the thirty-nine-year-old daughter of Carlos Valenzuela, *patron* of one of the most influential Castilian Spanish-land grant families in New Mexico whose vast land holdings, located northeast of Santa Fe, have been in the Valenzuela family for ten generations.

Following tradition, she gratified her father's wish to strengthen their bloodline by marrying another Castilian, Jose Martinez, a Navy pilot whose duty station was an aircraft carrier. Because he was stationed overseas so often, they chose to delay having children. Three months short of being discharged, Jose was killed during a training mission.

Heartbroken, Armida returned to the University of New Mexico, where she earned a doctorate in ethnology, the branch of anthropology devoted to the comparative studies of cultures. After graduation, the university offered her a position at the Taylor Museum, which she accepted. After years of hard work and dedication she's now the head curator of the museum.

Armida, who uses her maiden name, has a complexion almost flawless except for tiny telltale age lines at the corners of her eyes and mouth. Although she makes no attempt to flaunt her good looks, she's a tall striking looking woman. She usually wears her dark brown hair, with an unusual premature streak near the widow's peak on the right side, in a ponytail. On duty at the museum she favors Santa Fe style, long, gathered pleated skirts, embroidered or long-sleeved blouses, and high style leather boots. Her horn-rimmed glasses used only for close work are often perched on her head.

The tentative schedule complete, she reads her mail, holds a brief cell phone conversation with her editor, and is about to leave for the museum warehouse when her desk phone rings.

"Armida, are you coming home this weekend? I'm having some Navajo rugs brought up Saturday morning for your cousin's wedding gift. I'd like you to take a look at them. Can you make it?"

"Yes, Papa I'll be up Friday evening. Who's offering the rugs?"

"The Jaramillo gallery in Santa Fe."

Armida understands, without his saying so, why her father wants her to be there when he looks at new rugs. Recently imported fake Navajo rugs are causing real concern among collectors and museums. There are even unscrupulous dealers having old Pre-1900 style blankets replicated by Navajo weavers, and selling them as old weavings. Poor quality Navajo style Mexican rugs have also inundated the Navajo rug business, and as a consequence, she's relieved to hear that her father has contacted a reputable gallery. "Great," she says. "They handle good weavings. I look forward to seeing you, Papa."

"Bring up some fresh green chiles. We'll have chiles rellenos for breakfast. Ours are not quite ripe."

"I'll stop by Lucero's farm and have some roasted. *Te amo, Papa.*"

"*Y yo te amo, muchacha,*" Carlos replies.

Armida and her father have been very close since her mother's death when she was only thirteen. He raised her, assisted by a housekeeper, Juanita Garcia, who despite her love for the child, was a dominating sort of woman and kept young Armida under very close supervision. Now semi-retired, Juanita still lives at the rancho and helps care for Armida's father. Armida attended private Catholic schools until she entered UCLA where she graduated summa cum laude with a Bachelor's degree in anthropology. She transferred to the University of New Mexico for her Master's. Before marrying Jose, she thought she might talk her father into expanding the vineyard at the ranch and selling the wine. But like most men of his breeding, he has serious reservations about a women's place in the business world.

Although her work at the University is rewarding, when she isn't traveling, Armida spends as much time as possible at the Valenzuela ranch, riding the famous Jaramillo Palomino horses and working in the vineyard.

She glances at her watch, remembering that she has a date to help identify some old Navajo weavings in fifteen minutes.

Gathering up her briefcase and Palm Pilot, she hurries to the laboratory, a fully equipped facility that would be the envy of any forensic professional.

She joins Mary Chavez, a lab assistant, who's much like a younger sister to Armida. Mary's family has worked for the Valenzuelas since they both were babies. Mary's parents and her husband died years ago when a drunken driver crossed lanes just outside Taos and hit them head on. Mary, who was pregnant at the time, was also in the car but suffered only minor injuries. Soon after Mary's son Jesse was born, Armida helped her to get a job in the laboratory where she soon became one of the Taylor's top technicians.

As a team, Armida and Mary couple scientific and historic analysis to solve aging and ethnic origin mysteries. Whenever possible, Mary and Jesse spend weekends at the Valenzuela rancho with Armida's father. Jesse calls Carlos "Papa" just as Armida does, and Carlos's crazy about the boy. In Albuquerque, Mary shares an apartment near the campus with a divorced dispatcher for the police department and her three-year-old daughter. Since Mary works days and her roommate works nights, they're able to take care of each other's children.

Armida enters the lab Armida reflecting on how she never tires of looking at Navajo weavings. The valuable collection she and Mary are to inspect today is supposed to consist primarily of pre-1900 blankets. A wealthy widow of a local doctor has made the donation to the university in memory of her late husband. Armida hopes these weavings will turn out to be legitimate, but in one of the photos, submitted with the collection, she's noticed something that bothers her.

Once again her expertise is to be tested, a challenge she relishes.

CHAPTER 3
Santa Fe New Mexico

Miguel leaves Albuquerque early Saturday morning for the sixty-mile drive to Santa Fe. His drive on I-25 takes him along the Rio Grande River, past the Santo Domingo Pueblo. He arrives just as his gallery opens at nine. The gallery director, Paul Aragon, brings him current on the past week's sales activity, adding that Carlos Valenzuela wants to see a few small modern Navajo rugs for a wall display. He's giving the rugs to his niece as wedding gifts and he wants someone from the gallery to bring them to his ranch this morning. After helping Paul select six tapestry quality rugs, Miguel decides to show the rugs himself. Checking his mail, he returns a few phone calls, then loads three rugs by prize winning weavers and several other contemporary rugs into his van and leaves for the Valenzuela hacienda.

His trip takes him north through the little village of Chimayo, famous for colorful weavings created on horizontal Spanish type looms. He has four families of weavers there who regularly provide enough weavings for both of his galleries. His personal preference is for older Navajo blankets woven before 1900. Modern Navajo rugs bear little resemblance to old weavings but today's Chimayo weavings have remained much the same as the old ones. These weavings, often referred to as Rio Grande Textiles, are bright and colorful and he finds that interior decorators use them extensively.

Continuing along the eastern face of the Sange De Cristo mountain range to Penasco, he drives just south of the San Lorenzo Pueblo. Winding his way east over the Continental Divide, the narrow, meandering road takes him past thick timber stands and occasional large groves of aspen trees. The trip provides a scenic view of one of the most beautiful areas of New Mexico.

Further along the eastern slope, he sees the historic church of Saint Pellico and he pauses, as he often does, to visit the famous old church. Built between 1630 and 1641, the church features sixty-foot high ceilings and six-foot deep walls and is the centerpiece of the small community of Morphy. Because of the complete restoration of the beautiful eighteenth century murals in the early 1960's, the church has recently received a Presidential Historical Preservation Award. Miguel always finds the murals calming.

Back on the road, Miguel's thoughts turn to the manila envelope he found on the back seat of his van. There's no address on it, just a simple 'We Will Be In Contact' scrawled on the outside. Opening it he found a scrap of weaving enclosed in a protective plastic covering. Unlike any he's acquainted with, it's obviously fragile and very old. The scrap was an unusual color and made from what appeared to be unraveled wool, possibly Bayeta, the Spanish name for baize. Navajo weavers used this wool, which was manufactured in

England, for a limited time before the turn of the century.

Again and again as he drives through the mountains, his thoughts return to the scrap of fabric. He brought the scrap along today for no better reason than it continues to arouse his curiosity. He first thought it might not be Navajo. But the more he studied it, the more he became convinced it's an ancient example of Navajo or possibly Pueblo weaving.

When he's a few miles from the Valenzuela hacienda, Miguel calls Carlos Valenzuela on his cell phone. "Hola, Amigo. Miguel Jaramillo here. I'm about two miles from your casa. I should be there shortly."

Carlos's warm, familiar voice rings out. "Hola, Amigo. It will be good to see you again. Welcome to my casa."

The Valenzuela hacienda is like a small community with its numerous outbuildings bordered by low, red adobe walls that delineate each occupant's property line. Entering through a white stuccoed, arched entrance he notices the single word "Valenzuela" spelled out with inset red bricks. Hanging from the center of the arch is a metal replica of the ranch's famous brand, the Rocking V. Driving under the gate-less arch, he sees the Valenzuela ranch headquarters in the distance. The headquarters are a group of one-story buildings dominated by a long, low, terra cotta red adobe structure. A veranda runs the full length of the building with windows accented with bright blue frames. Dozens of red chile ristras hang, evenly spaced, under the long portal. To Miguel's left are stables, and to his right, rows of field corn with yellow tassels waving gently.

Closer to the hacienda he spots a field of ripening chile loaded with bright green pods.

When he drives up to the long building and parks in front of the main entrance, he spots Carlos's daughter, Armida, striding toward him. Miguel knows she is head curator of the Taylor Museum of Natural History at the University of New Mexico where last year he attended a lecture she gave on Pueblo Indian Textiles. This morning she's wearing high waisted, tight, tan riding britches, black leather boots, and a blue silk-embroidered blouse. Her long black hair drawn back in a ponytail.

Miguel is more than a little surprised to realize the success with which Armida was able to conceal her sexuality the night of her lecture with her severely cut suit and horn-rimmed glasses. The voluptuous beauty that moves briskly toward him this morning looks nothing like the prim, proper Castilian matron he heard speak that evening.

Armida greets him by extending her hand as he steps down from the van. Without hesitation he bends and brushes her knuckles lightly with his lips.

"*Bueños Dias, Dõna* Valenzuela."

Smiling easily, she replies, "*Bueños Dias, Senõr* Jaramillo. We'll probably find my father in the garden. Please follow me."

Entering the house through eight-foot high antique rough-hewn doors, they follow a dramatic red tiled corridor passing by a white, adobe-walled room filled with antiques and dominated by a rounded adobe fireplace. On the floor Miguel recognizes the three large Navajo rugs as having come from the Jaramillo gallery. Beautifully framed portraits of three generations of the

Valenzuela family and numerous paintings by famous artists including Joseph Henry Sharp, Oscar E. Berninghouse and Irvin Couse of the Taos Society of Artists hang on the walls. Through an archway to his right is a formal paneled dining room with a long dining table that can easily accommodate two dozen guests and is surrounded by high-backed chairs of various upholstered velvet.

Stopping at the third door on the right, Armida indicates they should enter. A whiff of spice brings back memories of the first time Miguel, as a young man, visited this hacienda with his father. In the center of the beautiful open courtyard stands an elegant water fountain next to a small, well cared for vegetable garden a elderly white-haired Valenzuela is bent over a row of cilantro, a pungent herb used so frequently in New Mexico cuisine.

Armida's father spots them, removes his gloves and lays aside his wicker basket. "Hola, Amigo." he greets Miguel. "Welcome, to mi *casa*."

The warmth in Carlos Valenzuela's greeting indicates he is pleased Miguel has decided to come himself. Miguel's father was a friend of the Valenzuela family for many years and although Miguel has had limited personal contact with the old patron, he's fully aware that this is one of the most important men in the Hispanic community.

Carlos's a large man, heavy and full at the belt, with penetrating eyes and a handlebar mustache.

"Would you care for something to drink?" he asks, in a strong tenor voice "Some excellent Bordeaux from my vineyard, perhaps?"

The Valenzuela vineyard is noted for being established long before the first vines were planted in California and providing the sacramental wines used in the Old Church of Saint Dellico.

Miguel replies warmly, "Yes, of course."

Carlos smiles approvingly and whispers something in the ear of an attractive, slightly built young woman in a squaw dress and beaded moccasins who has been lingering in the hallway. When she and Armida disappear into the house, Carlos suggests he and Miguel retire to the study.

Miguel's struck by the sheer opulence of the room in which the art objects alone are clearly worth a fortune. Paintings hang on every available space of the whitewashed walls, and a beautiful Tiffany stained-glass wisteria lamp stands behind a leather couch that can easily seat six. Three large, tan leather chairs are strategically located opposite the couch. One wall is dominated by floor to ceiling bookcases completely filled with calfskin bound volumes.

He notices a bronze of a matador dramatically poised over a bull on a pedestal in one corner. Other bronzes include a rare 'Bronco Buster' by Frederick Remington. Perched on a shelf overlooking the room is a magnificent mounted Great Horned owl with outstretched wings. Spectacular earth tone Navajo rugs from the Two Grey Hills area cover most of the tile floor and several large garishly colored Zuni Clown Kachina dolls are carefully placed here and there. The paintings include two Indian portraits by Sharp, a pencil study of an Indian by W.R. Leigh and a dramatic C.M. Russell of a buffalo hunt that Miguel remembers Carlos bought from his father a few years before.

The room with its curious mixture of Spanish influence and Western Americana antiques gives Miguel further insight into the sophisticated taste of Carlos Valenzuela. Miguel knows the wealthy old patron was educated at the University of Seville and traveled the world before coming here to rule the family's domain with an iron fist. Carlos is both respected and feared in the community and his support is critical for those wishing to be elected to public office in the county.

Indicating a huge leather couch, Carlos sits opposite Miguel in one of the large chairs before he asks after Miguel's health and comments on the drought that has plagued the area for three years. Moments later, the young woman, accompanied by Armida enters the room, carrying a deep silver tray that holds glasses and a bottle of wine. After carefully placing it on a large wood desk, she leaves the room while Armida takes a seat in the chair next to her father.

Picking up a corkscrew from the tray, Carlos deftly removes the cork from the wine bottle and pours a small quantity into one of the glasses. He swirls the glass, holds it to his nose, inhales the aroma and takes a sip. Satisfied with the selection, he pours three glasses and proposes a toast to Miguel's health, receiving Miguel's compliments with obvious pleasure. Picking up the bottle and noting the year, Armida offers, "I hope this year's Merlot compares. This came from one of our finest pressings."

"There's every indication it will be," adds Carlos.

Watching the two interact, Miguel realizes how easily they blend into the décor of the room and seem to compliment it. Their breeding is evident and he can't help but feel a little out of place. After some small talk and another glass of Valenzuela's finest, Miguel asks, "When is your niece's wedding?"

"Oh, not for a few weeks," the old man replies. "But since Armida's home for a couple of days, I've asked her to look at what you might have to offer. As you might imagine, I value her opinion."

"I heard one of Armida's presentations at the Taylor last year," Miguel says, "and you have every reason to do so."

Carlos smiles approvingly at the compliment then glances at Armida. "I'm very proud of her accomplishments, but her work leaves her little time for the vineyard."

"Oh Papa I'm finished with the grant now and will be home more."

Ignoring Armida, Carlos looks at Miguel. "How many rugs did you bring?"

As for Armida, she makes no comment to her father's dig. "I've selected six," declares Miguel, setting his glass down "I think you'll like them. They're some of the finest we have here in Santa Fe. However, if none of them strike your fancy, perhaps we have something you would like in our Albuquerque gallery. Would you like to see them now?"

"Of course. Bring them in," Carlos replies. "Armida, would you give him a hand?"

Outside at his van, Miguel opens the back doors and removes a collapsible cart. Moving it around to the side of the van, he opens the sliding door and starts to remove the Navajos. Standing by, Armida watches as he meticulously stacks the rugs, each carefully wrapped in a protective cotton cover. He then places his briefcase on the bottom shelf.

"Looks like you've done this before."

Miguel senses that Armida is clearly at ease with him and feels she is warming up to his presence.

He replies, "Once or twice," grinning as he closes the van door and pushes the cart toward the hacienda.

Back in the library, Miguel removes each weaving from its cover and carefully spreads it out on the floor. He has purposely selected contemporary pieces to show the old patron. Weavings that are varied in both style and color. Two are intricate Burnt Water patterns featuring natural earth tone colors and delicate weaving. Another is a bold, geometric patterned, brown and black Two Grey Hills, and the final three feature contemporary designs by famous weavers known to Armida. One of the weaver's weavings was displayed last year in a showing of contemporary weaving at the Taylor.

Only when all the rugs are displayed does Armida look them over carefully. Her eyes narrow in a way that reminds Miguel that nothing is going to get by her. Clearly she will be a shrewd bargainer. Miguel watches as she murmurs something to her father and picks one up, the beautiful little Two Grey Hills done by a prize-winning weaver.

"Who is the weaver?" Armida asks?

"Mary Yazzi. It's one of her best."

"Really?"

There's nothing condescending in the way she replies, although he realizes she's assessing him as well as the rugs.

"How much for this little one and the last one you have there?" Carlos asks, taking the weaving from Armida.

Miguel's not surprised that Armida has easily identified the two best pieces in the group, the second rug she has selected is a pictorial featuring eight Ye'iis. Taking his Palm Pilot from the brief case, he punches in the numbers.

"Your daughter has excellent taste." he tells Carlos.

"She has selected two of my finest. They come to $6,200.00. Or would you prefer that I price them separately?"

"I need a little more time." Carlos tells him returning to his examination of the Two Grey. "I'll let you know. If you have a few minutes, perhaps Armida could show you around our hacienda."

As they leave the house together, Armida remembers the first time she saw Miguel, when she and her father visited the Jaramillo gallery. She thought him extraordinarily handsome.   Miguel's father waited on them that day. However, she had been unable to keep her gaze off Miguel as he arranged a display of Santa Clara pottery. And although he hadn't acknowledged her, she was certain he had noticed her that day as well.

The years have been good to him. He's even more handsome now than he was then. Celibate since Jose's death, Armida finds herself strangely aroused as she leads him to the stables, with its dozens of stalls and white-boarded corrals.

She stops to introduce him to their finest stud. The Valenzuela family is famous not only for their vineyards but also for their Palominos. The best of their best is a beautiful, golden tan stallion whose long, flaxen mane and tail are magnificent. A dramatic piece of horseflesh, the stud prances around in the stall and comes snorting up to the half-door. Armida takes a sugar cube from her pocket and hands it to Miguel.

"Hold this in the palm of your hand so he can see it," she tells him.

"I thought all stallions were mean." Miguel offers, as the stallion's warm, soft muzzle brushes his palm and retrieves the cube. "But he seems gentle enough."

"Oh, Carlos's Golden Boy is a softy when there isn't a mare around. But when there is, you'd better stay clear. Then he's all business."

Miguel sees the pride in Armida's eyes as she speaks about the animal, and is sure this is the same mount she was astride last fall in the county fair parade. She was a glorious sight to see. Dressed in a black Spanish matron's outfit, she rode easily on a saddle studded with silver conchas that contrasted beautifully with the golden color of the stallion. And now here she is beside him.

His breath quickens a little, as he ponders the deep social and cultural gap between the old Castilian families of New Mexico and the more recent Mexican arrivals like his own family. He's well aware of a true class distinction that exists between them. But Armida really appeals to him, not only because of her beauty but perhaps because he's always been drawn to older women.

As the tour continues, Miguel can't help but be impressed by what he's sure is some of the finest Palomino breeding stock in New Mexico.

At the end of the corrals, the famous Valenzuela vineyard comes into full view. Hidden from the road in front of the hacienda, the long rows of vines stretch down the valley behind the Valenzuela complex. Miguel's not prepared for the number of rows of vines all neatly clinging to their support frames. The vineyard must easily cover two hundred acres.

"Are all these grapes for your own use?" he asks.

Armida laughs, "Hardly. We sell what we don't process for wine. We primarily grow Merlot. They're premium red-wine grapes and very much in demand for blending with the Cabernet Sauvignon. Merlot produces a richly complex Bordeaux style wine. You just enjoyed a glass."

Armida looks past him into the distance. "Someday I hope to produce many more varieties and expand our winery."

"Everyone should have a dream," Miguel tells her, surprised by her willingness to share her plans for the future. On the one hand he senses a detachment that can never be penetrated, although at the same time, he feels as though they have known each other for a long time.

"What's yours?" asks Armida.

"I haven't given it much thought," he says with a shrug. "I guess it's the same as any man's. A nice home, a wife and children. But I've been too busy with the galleries to think seriously about marriage. Besides, I haven't found the right lady."

The truth is, something always forges a distance between Miguel and any woman who starts to act as if she's looking for a husband. Lately, however, just before he goes to sleep, he has begun to wonder if he's destined to be a bachelor forever. But this woman stirs something inside him.

"And you?" he says, looking deep into Armida's blue eyes.

For a brief second she's startled. It's almost as though Miguel can see into her soul. This man's gaze is so direct, so immediate, so intimate, that Armida finds herself blushing. "Perhaps we should go back," she says crisply. "My father should have made his decision by now."

"Before I leave, I have something in the van I'd like you to see," Miguel says as they approach the hacienda. She's about to answer when her father joins them.

"Did you enjoy your tour?" Carlos asks.

"Yes, thank you. You have a beautiful place," Miguel replies. Glancing at Armida, he adds, "Your daughter is an excellent tour guide."

"One day this will all be hers." Carlos tells him.

"Armida loves our rancho. I only wish we would see more of her. For the last couple of years the only time she seems to be here is when we're harvesting the grapes."

"Oh, Father," Armida says, "that's not completely true. I'm here almost every weekend."

Noting the tension in their exchange, Miguel remembers his father's advice about closing a sale and attempts to change the subject. "Have you decided which rugs you like?" he asks the old man.

Carlos says nothing. But when they reach the study, Miguel sees four of the Navajos, carefully returned to their cotton wrappings, and placed on the cart while the two rugs that Armida selected are nowhere to be seen.

"I'll give you five thousand and two cases of the wine you tasted, for the two rugs my daughter likes," the old man says brusquely.

"I wish I could," Miguel replies. "Perhaps we should look again at some of the others I brought. Let me check."

"Fifty five-hundred and the wine." Carlos says. "My final offer."

"I'll send you a bill," Miguel tells him after a pause. "I appreciate your business and I thank you for calling our gallery. You're a valued customer and I'm pleased you like my selections."

"You're a lot like your father," Carlos replies. "I miss him. He was a good man, and we spent much time together. Thank you for coming, I'll send the wine. Please visit us again. Armida will see you out. Adios, Senõr Jaramillo"

"What did you want to show me?" Armida asks, following him out the door onto the tile porch, now scorching hot in the August sun.

"It's in the van," he tells her. "Let me get the envelope."

After studying the scrap of weaving intently, Armida asks if he had brought gloves and when he finds them, she carefully removes the scrap of weaving from the plastic covering. From her expression Miguel can tell she's puzzled.

"Do you have a glass?"

Miguel retrieves a jeweler's eyepiece from his briefcase. Without comment, she uses it to study the weaving. "It's a corner piece, which still has remnants of the original tassel, apparently roughly cut from a larger weaving. Where in the world did you come up with this?" she finally asks.

"I'm afraid I can't say at the moment." Miguel tells her. "Have you ever seen anything like it?"

"I believe I have." Armida says, barely able to conceal her excitement. "But I would need to study it further."

Miguel places the scrap back in his briefcase.

"I may be able to you tell you where it came from in a few days," he says.

"Where else have you seen something like this?"

They were sparring now. Armida is hesitant to disclose what she thinks until Miguel is more forthcoming about the source. She recognizes the scrap as being very similar to the earliest known examples of Navajo weaving that the museum has in its own collection. The examples are fragments from the Massacre Cave, Canyon de Chelly discovery and are considered priceless. Armida tries to remain calm by reminds herself the fragments in the museum were woven with a striped pattern, while this one sports an unusual design pattern that she does not recognize. Still, there appears to be no questioning the weaving is the same material and style.

"Is there any chance I might have it for a little while?" she asks Miguel. "I need to do some testing to confirm a few things."

"I'm not sure I can do that." he tells her. "I'll have to think about it. Can't you tell me what you think it is?"

Armida decides to disclose her suspicions. After all, it was important that he trusts her, as well as understands he might have something of great value here. Once having seen the scrap, she finds she does not want to let it out of her sight.

"Are you familiar with the discovery of early textiles found in Massacre Cave?" she asks.

"Yes, I am," he says frowning. "I recently visited Canyon de Chelly. But what does the cave have to do with this?"

"Examples of the cache of textiles found there are now in museums all over the world." Armida informs him. "We have two striped samples in our collection which are considered the earliest known examples of Navajo textiles. I feel there is a good chance your piece may even be older, but it will take some testing, possibly D.N.A. and carbon dating to verify my opinion. The point is, what you have here could be a very rare and significant find."

Standing there thunderstruck, Miguel never dreamed the old scrap could be something of this magnitude, but he respects Armida's opinion. After all, she's one of the nation's top experts on Native American textiles.

"How long would you need to have the piece?"

"I would think about a week," she tells him, her voice crisp, again businesslike.

Miguel's uncomfortably aware of how easily she moves from one persona to another. Now she is all professionalism, a stranger to him again.

"The D.N.A. tests would take the longest," she continues. "I need to verify the wool and there also appears to be some cotton content. The dyes used will be fairly simple to determine, but the breed of sheep that produced the wool and the cotton variety will take the longest. The university will, of course, cover any costs. But I will need a release from you. If the scrap is what I think it is, I would certainly want to publish my findings. What do you say?"

Miguel is reeling from her hypothesis, and says, "Let me think on it," "I'll get back to you soon, I promise."

He can't tell her that he now has real concerns about the scrap. Only three weeks ago he testified at the trial of a man who was convicted under the Antiquities Act. The man had been found with illegal Native American pottery dug on the reservation land. Without knowing where this scrap came from Miguel doesn't feel he dares let Armida examine it at great length for fear this too could have been obtained illegally. First he needs to try to find out who left it with him. The last thing he needs is to get her mixed up in a scandal involving Indian artifacts.

All the way back to Santa Fe, Miguel recounts what has just happened. *Who gave him such a rare weaving? Why him? And when would he hear from them again?*

CHAPTER 4
Albuquerque

Armida's thoughts center on the past weekend at the Valenzuela Ranch as she takes a break from detailed cataloging of the university's new acquisitions. Her father's comments to Miguel about her absences were well taken. For the past few months, she really hasn't been home as much as she would have liked and she did miss working in the vineyard. No matter how much her professional life absorbs her attention, the family vineyard is her first love and perhaps will always be what she cares about most. The fact that she and her husband elected not to have children disappointed her father deeply and she understands.

Of course it's important to him that there are grandchildren to inherit the family holdings. Perhaps since she's hasn't provided him with heirs, it's impossible to convince him how important it is to expand the vineyard. Lately, it seems one of these two issues is the subject of almost every conversation they have.

Her thoughts are interrupted, by the ringing of her phone.

"*Bueños Dias*, *Dõna*. Miguel Jaramillo here. Do you have a minute?"

Armida is a little surprised he has called so quickly. When they parted Saturday, she was under the impression it might be some time before he contacted her.

"*Buenõs Dias, Señor*," she replies. "What can I do for you?"

"I'll be in Albuquerque for a few days this week. I've spoken with my attorney and he sees no problem in allowing you to examine the weaving. I was only concerned because I didn't know the source.

There's always the possibility that the scrap could be from stolen or illegal goods and I didn't want to cause you any trouble. How about lunch? What does your schedule look like?"

Armida glances at her appointment book. "I can get away for lunch tomorrow or Wednesday. What suits you?"

"How about tomorrow at Dee's in the Old Town Plaza? Say 11:30?"

"Sounds good to me. I love their chicken fajitas."

"*Bueno*. I'll set it up."

It's strange she feels so drawn to this young man. Granted he's handsome, but she doesn't even know him. But there's something about the way he looks at her, so deep and penetrating. As she leans back into her high-backed chair, she recalls how good he smelled at the ranch and the soft touch of his warm lips as they brushed her knuckles. Thoughts like this could mean she's going to have a real problem with this attractive man. He brings back feelings she hasn't experienced since Jose's death. But she has no time and no plans for getting involved. Especially not with a young Latino like Miguel. My God! What would her father say?" She knows that if and when she chooses to remarry, she will be limited to a Spanish-speaking man of equal social status. It's questionable that her father would ever settle for a Latino as a son-in-law. Then, realizing she will be late for a staff meeting if she doesn't hurry, she gathers her notes and leaves. Time enough to worry about how she feels about this new man in her life.

Miguel arrives at Dee's Mexican Restaurant in Albuquerque's Old Town Plaza at 11:25 a.m. While waiting for Armida to arrive, he notices a black sedan cruising around the plaza, apparently looking for a parking space. It occurs to him this is the third time in the last three days he's noticed the black sedan with the dented door. *Strange,* he thinks. But then forgets about it as he sees Armida coming briskly toward him. Once again her hips are swaying, her breasts bouncing, the outline of her nipples faintly visible. Miguel catches a glimpse of her profile as someone whistles at her from a passing pickup truck. She turns her head to stare him down and her Castilian Spanish heritage has never been more evident. Her chiseled features, high cheekbones, dominated by a straight nose, full lips and a proud jaw are strong, while at the same time somehow soft and quite feminine. And then there is her air of sophistication. She approaches him looking like a model on the runway of a clothing fashion show, a lovely sight to behold.

"*Buenõs Dias, Senõr.* Have you waited long?"

"I just arrived, *Dõna,*" Miguel says, bending to kiss her fingers.

"Thanks for coming."

They're seated in the outdoor patio among an array of great red clay pots bursting with scarlet geraniums, which assails their senses with beauty and fragrance. In short order they are served tortilla chips, salsa and iced tea. Miguel asks. "What are you working on at the Taylor?"

"I've completed a one-year project and written a new book on the history of Navajo rugs," Armida replies. "It's a guide to identifying and dating weavings by means of their materials. I feel this is the single most important clue to the dating a rug's manufacture. I turned it over to the publishers last week and I'm back at the computer cataloging our collection. Are you familiar with our collection?"

"Of course," Miguel replies. I spent many hours there as a young man. I was a history major and also did research for my father. He was often busy with the galleries and used me to do some of his leg work."

"Our computerization is a little behind some of the museums I visited for my research," Armida tells him, "so I'll probably be working full time in this area for a while."

Miguel finds her delightfully animated as she describes her work on the fellowship and she's mesmerizing as she describes the tons of weavings and rugs she studied while she traced the weaving history of a dynamic race of people. Armida possesses a depth of knowledge and a memory for detail that he can hardly believe. And it seems natural that she, like Miguel, is fascinated with the history and crafts of the Navajos. He listens intently to the details of the weavings she inspected in various museums. Since joining his father, he has purchased and sold hundreds of them but remembers distinctly only some of the rarest, like the Second Phase Pattern wearing blanket he purchased for sixteen-hundred dollars and sold for five-thousand. But Armida's memory is astonishing and Miguel finds it obvious that her opinions are based on a historical perspective while his are generally commercial.

He can't recall ever meeting anyone like her. As any good conversationalist would, he listens quietly while she speaks, prompting her now and then with questions, a practice he has perfected over many years. Today he's learning a great deal about this lady.

"Did you bring the weaving scrap?" She asks when they finish lunch.

Miguel replies, "Yes, of course." and motions for the waiter to bring their check. "It's in my van, right down the street."

"Unfortunately, I've got a meeting," Armida says, looking at her watch. "I've got to hustle along."

When they arrive at the van, Miguel hands her the plastic envelope, which contains the weaving scrap and gives her his card.

"Please call as soon as you determine its origin," he says.

"I'll let you know right away." replies Armida, her warm smile indicating her pleasure. "Thanks for letting me have a chance to examine it. I enjoyed lunch. Let's do it again."

***

As they part, the strange little man, looking again like a homeless person, sits on a bench across the street observing them, and after making a few notes in his black book, he limps back to his black sedan and places a call on his cell phone. Until now, this has been a simple job for Armando Peralta. All he has to do is watch Miguel Jaramillo and report by phone to his client at least once a day.

At his age, this kind of surveillance is the only type of work he takes. In his youth, he handled a lot of tough assignments, but those days are gone. Now the Garcia Detective Agency calls him only for easy jobs. The years have taken their toll, and as he makes notes in his little book, the pain comes surging back. His left leg and his back have never been the same since a drunk broadsided him, and he's rarely able to stand erect for long unless he takes his medicine. He doesn't like to take it as it affects his mind and is addictive. He really doesn't need to work because he has always been frugal, and the accident settlement was a generous one. But no amount of money is worth the pain he now is forced to endure. So he takes this kind of easy job because he likes to get out once in a while.

So far, this assignment has actually been boring, with nothing worth reporting. Following his client's clear instructions, and using some of his old skills, he slipped an envelope into Miguel's van at the Crownpoint auction. Since then he's simply followed the gallery owner around as he goes about his business. Today is the first time Miguel has appeared to have any personal life and Armando approves. The señorita with him is quite a picture. When the couple arrived at Miguel's van, Armando recognized the envelope Miguel handed her and knows immediately he better find out more about Miguel's lunch date. With a choice to make, he quickly decides to follow the lady.

When she pulls into the parking lot at the Taylor museum, Armando is right behind, following her inside, he joins her on the elevator which takes them to the third floor offices. As they leave the elevator, he hears another woman greet her by her first name and the rest is easy. Armando simply checks the staff directory and returns to his car to again call his client and make his report.

"Miguel Jaramillo gave the envelope I placed in the van at Crownpoint to a curator at the University of New Mexico's Taylor Museum," he reports.

"I want a complete rundown on the curator." the curt voice snarls. "I mean complete and I want it fast. Do you understand?"

"Yes, of course." Armando replies. "I'll get on it right away. Do you still want me to keep Jaramillo under surveillance?"

"Certainly. Can't you do both?"

"Of course."

"Call as soon as you have something."

Armando calls the agency and tells them to do a background check, pronto! Then he returns to the Jaramillo gallery on the plaza in Old Town and takes up a surveillance post under a huge Mimosa tree on the outer edge of the plaza. He's not sure Miguel has returned to the gallery, until a moment later when he sees him setting up a new display of old Apache baskets in the gallery window. Satisfied, Armando moves into position on a bench across the street and tries to relax, shaded from the bright New Mexico sun by the old tree. As he leans back, he hears the soft whirring of wings and spots the bright colored flashes of two male hummingbirds as they stage a mock dogfight for exclusive rights to a red bottomed feeder on a low hanging branch nearby.

***

Putting the finishing touches to the new display, Miguel returns to his office on the mezzanine above the gallery floor. Seated at his desk, he can look through a window to his right, down upon the gallery floor. Like his father, when time permits, he likes to deal with some of the gallery's better customers personally. Although the staff is capable, Miguel's aware that most wealthy customers prefer to deal with the owner, feeling no doubt, that they will get a better value that way.

Today has been an exciting one for him. The lunch with Armida was even more special than he expected and he realizes that this lady, although at least six- maybe more- years his senior, is someone who triggers new feelings in him. He enjoys a long-standing arrangement with the young divorcee of a Hollywood producer, which satisfies both of their sexual needs. But both of them know the arrangement is out of the public temporary at best. Particularly since the divorcee spends only about half of her time in her second home in Santa Fe. Theirs is a very private affair. She prefers to stay out of the limelight, and Miguel finds this a satisfying arrangement and respects her wishes. But now, although their cultural and age differences might pose a problem, he feels he has picked up encouraging vibes from Armida Sitting back in his chair he's enjoying the memories of their lunch when he spots a valued customer come in and hurries down to greet him. For the moment Armida disappears from his thoughts as the salesman in him takes over.

    Outside on his bench in the plaza, the warm New Mexico temperature has eased some of the old private detective's pain, and he's asleep. Suddenly Armando is awakened by a clap of thunder, as a bolt of lightning strikes the Mimosa tree above him. Moments later, a late afternoon shower soaks him as he scurries to his car. He glances toward the Jaramillo Gallery and notes that Miguel appears to be no where in site.

***

    At four in the afternoon, Armida decides to take the weaving scrap down to the lab where she finds Mary Chavez looking at some slides. Armida greets her, "Hi! Got a few minutes to look at a sample?" "Of course. What do we have?"

    Mary is a little on the heavy side, but attractive. She has large eyes with long eyelashes, a flawless complexion and always appears freshly scrubbed. Armida loves working with her; they make a good team.

    When Armida brings out the weaving scrap, they both agree that it may prove to be a tough one to identify. They start with a spectral examination. Using some of the latest and best equipment, the results are compared to the museum's vast base of computerized standards.

    Once the dyes and wool types are identified, Armida's almost photographic memory supplies the stylistic elements needed to classify the sample. Working side by side, they take a microscopic look at the warp. Armida knows that Navajo weavers add the weft after the warp of a weaving in order to construct it as a complete separate textile. Since warp materials and techniques varied for maintaining the strength and form of a weaving, this analysis is vital in determining the origin of any particular sample.

    Armida also knows that occasionally certain weavers were known to add materials to different areas of the warp textile. It's a standard procedure in the laboratory to use microphotographs to document warp yarn types and variation. These are utilized to determine the consistency of any materials present and to detect any modifications including any blending caused by carting, raveling, and the use of commercial or hand spun yarns. The process is long and painstaking, but like Mary, Armida loves the work. She feels like a detective after successfully identifying a weaving's origin.

    The pair work most of the afternoon with only a short break for supper until finally the wool is identified as hand carded Churros.

    When the Spanish explorer Coronado arrived in New Mexico in 1540, he introduced Churros sheep to the Southwest.   The Navajos initially accumulated their flocks by trade or raids on Spanish ranches and Pueblo Indian farms. Since Armida believes the Navajos learned how to weave from the Pueblo Indians, who used cotton before the Spanish arrived, she feels it is very likely this particular weaving dates later than the mid-fifteen-hundreds. Closer inspection also determines that no other materials have been used in the weaving.

The most telling discovery is that no synthetic dyes have been used. All the dyes in the scrap are natural. That narrows their search considerably. Armida becomes more and more excited as she finally realizes they are looking at a piece of Navajo weaving which may predate any she knows. Clearly the scrap is a rare find and hopefully only a small part of a priceless wearing blanket which could be from about 1700 or possibly earlier, making it one of the earliest know examples of Navajo weaving. Mary and Armida are both elated. They are also dead tired.

Armida's tempted to give Miguel a call with their results, but it's very late and she decides to wait until the morning. Exhausted, she thanks Mary for staying late and heads for the parking lot.

CHAPTER 5
Roswell New Mexico

Miguel finds the call from the auctioneer a bit of a surprise. His impression was that the Jason Well's estate would be sold in September, but he was obviously wrong. If he's going to get an advance peek at the estate, he will have to be in Roswell today.

The early Friday morning traffic is light as he drives south from Albuquerque on I-25. His trip takes him along the Rio Grande River past the Isleta Indian Reservation and the old community of Belen, toward Socorro. Off to his left, tall trees grow beside the Rio Grande River forming a lush green backdrop to fertile fields of alfalfa blooms and ripening red chile crops being harvested by Mexican stoop labor. As he drives past the bent figures, he can't help but wonder if his grandparents worked these same fields. He often thinks of them and wonders how they were able to spend long hours working the land in New Mexico's torrid sun.

Seventy-five miles south of Albuquerque he turns east on highway 380. After crossing the Rio Grande River, the scenery quickly changes as he makes his way through the rugged, almost barren land, until after traveling up and over the Sierra Obscura range, he drops lower and cruises past the rugged, black, volcanic national recreation area know as the Valley of Fire.

Continuing east, he soon finds himself in gentle rolling hills, where little old towns like Carrizozo are nestled. He then winds his way through the Capitan Mountains into Lincoln County. Here from 1878 to 1881, a lawless war between merchants, homesteaders and cattlemen attracted notorious members of the criminal element, the most celebrated being Billy the Kid. Finally he emerges out of the mountains onto the barren plains that were once part of the famous Chisum Ranch. As he continues on Eastward, the city of Roswell appears.

During World War II, Roswell was the home of Walker Air Force Base, a SAC facility that is now closed. Smiling, Miguel remembers Roswell's current claim to fame centers around a controversial UFO crash in 1947. The reported crash, a few miles north of Roswell, is thought by many to be the only incident in which alien bodies have been discovered. Fifty plus years later, recurring charges of a government cover-up persist and major unresolved questions still surround the crash. Each year, thousands of people from all over the world, many of them on their way to the famous Carlsbad Caverns south of Roswell, pause to visit the International UFO Museum in Roswell.

The Jason Well's estate, which is to be auctioned in a couple weeks, is a significant one. Although no member of the family currently resides in

Roswell, the family was once one of Roswell's oldest and wealthiest. Now the only living heir is Grace Well, a spinster who teaches English at an eastern university and who has come to Roswell to settle the estate and meet with Miguel on Friday. He's aware that she has also indicated to the auctioneer that she's willing to consider some private sales in advance of the actual public auction, a practice frowned upon by tax collectors but fairly common in estate sales.

Since Ms. Well is scheduled to leave before the auction, Miguel knows he will need to work fast. Jason Well, a wealthy West Texas oilman whose passion for Indian artifacts was well known, collected the items that Miguel is interested in at the turn of the century. In preparation for the auction, Ms. Well has retrieved some of the finest items in the Well's collection from museums, where for years they were on loan. Miguel's sure when the bidding starts, some of those same museums will be among the bidders. Since museums are known to pay outrageous prices for items they might need to complete a particular collection; Miguel is pleased to have a chance for an advance purchase.

Jason Well's particular interest was in early Navajo weavings and rugs and Miguel is anxious to see the fruits of the elder Well's labor and excited at the possibility of obtaining a number of important pieces. In preparation, he's made arrangements for the Roswell branch of his bank to honor a significant request for cash should he be fortunate enough to be successful with Grace Well. This buy could be important if he decides to open a third gallery in Las Vegas.

Because of the burgeoning housing boom in the West, the Navajo weaving market is particularly hot. Indian artifacts used to adorn new Pueblo style homes bring some of the best known interior decorators to his galleries on a regular basis.

Arriving in time to check into a motel. Miguel freshens up then dresses carefully in a custom-made Western suit, and an expensive set of matching Zuni turquoise inlaid pieces. The set consists of a watch band, bolo tie, ring, and belt buckle. He also sports rattlesnake hide boots. Like his father before him, he always takes special care to look successful when he is in public. Today may be a very big day. Miguel is ready.

He finds little difficulty locating the Well's home since it's on a corner lot, right in the center of Roswell's Historic District. Here stately, turn-of-the-century homes line the street. But the Well's home is by far the largest. Beautifully preserved, it's a gloriously painted old lady, done up in various shades, of lavender, turquoise, yellow, and gray.

At the front door, the auctioneer, Colonel Briggs, the "Colonel" part being an honorary Kentucky title, greets Miguel. Once inside, Miguel realizes the bidders in this auction are in for a treat. The home, a spectacular view into Roswell's past, is everything he anticipated and more. Everywhere he looks there are antiques, paintings, and silver pieces he knows will command top dollar prices.

Leading him through a hallway into a large study, Colonel Briggs introduces Miguel to Grace Well, a tall, distinguished looking woman with blue-white hair who after shaking his hand, asks if they would like some coffee. She serves coffee and cookies in an elegant dinning room that contains a fortune in antique furniture and paintings by early American landscape painters. Ms. Well then leads the way back through a large kitchen out the back door to a coach house. The interior of which is a like giant red cedar-lined closet. One entire side contains deep floor to ceiling racks which hold dozens of rolled up weavings of all sizes.

Each rack features an inventory and condition list stapled on the end. By Miguel's quick estimate, there are at least two hundred weavings on the racks. On the left side of the room are dozens of smaller racks, which contain pottery, Kachina dolls, baskets, various beaded items and other artifacts. In the center of the room, between the racks, are two eight-foot folding tables and three standing lamps. There are also several chairs, ladders, three file cabinets and an old roll top desk against the far wall. The place is an immaculately clean museum warehouse

"Please take what time you need to look around," Ms. Well says, "then we'll discuss what you would like to see."

Miguel feels as though he's a child in a candy store. He takes his time, sauntering slowly past each rack, stopping to study the inventory lists which state the size, type, condition and year acquired for each of the rolled weavings housed on the rack. At every stop, he also studies any exposed surfaces of the weavings. Occasionally he takes out his eyeglass to more closely inspect a particular weaving.

His heart suddenly skips a beat as he reads "Early First Phase Chief's Ute 1885" on one of the lists. Attempting to suppress his excitement, he notes the condition indicted on the listing, moves past the Ute and continues casually walking through the racks. Realizing that this may be the best opportunity he'll ever have to acquire some really valuable weavings, he struggles to remain calm.

Struggling to contain his emotions he says, "This is a very nice collection, I'd like to get a good look. It may take some time, but I'm sure I can use a number of them. What do you two have in mind?" Miguel includes the Colonel because he's the one making this advance buy possible.

"I've got a couple of young men who would be available to help in the morning," the colonel says as they take seats around the table. "How about an early start? Is 7:00 a.m. satisfactory?"

Pleased that he is once again taking charge, the Colonel leans back in his chair with a satisfied smile as Miguel agrees and offers to have one of his staff fly in to assist them.

Looking directly at Miguel, Ms. Well says, "The Colonel tells me you're a reputable dealer. I'm aware these are very valuable but I really have no idea what they are worth on today's market. Colonel Briggs indicated you might be willing to pay cash. Is this true Mr. Jaramillo?"

"Our firm is one of the oldest in New Mexico. My father was in the business for many years. Suddenly it's important that she understand something about his credentials.

"I've been raised in it. I'm willing to pay a fair, wholesale price, but one that allows me to make a profit. I'll leave it up to you to say "yea" or "nay" to any price I offer. I may also choose a couple of other items for my personal collection. I'll identify those items. There's also another possibility. If you wish, I can give you a figure for all the weavings except for an appropriate number of pieces to be offered at the auction. I realize if you've already advertised this auction and bidders will expect some weavings to be offered."

"What do you think?" Ms. Well asks the Colonel.

"I would like to have at least fifty or so for the sale," he tells her. "The rest can be sold as a lot if you wish. I've dealt with Miguel on a number of occasions and I know him to be fair. His reputation is well known, and he'll keep this pre-sale confidential. I would of course, ask for my normal commission on the lot, also to be paid in cash."

That said, he waits. The room grows quiet. All three of them know that what they are doing could be considered highly unethical.

"I believe it's worth considering," says Ms. Well quietly, looking directly at Miguel. "Do you have any idea what you might be prepared to offer for the lot?" It's tough to estimate, until I get to spend some more time with them, but I have around one hundred thousand to spend," he offers.

The room is quiet again. Then Ms. Well rises slowly from her chair. With arms folded, she paces back and forth. After what seems to be an interminable time, she leans toward Miguel and places both hands on the table. "I would consider one hundred fifty thousand if you agree to leave at least fifty pieces for sale at the auction. If you are prepared to pay cash and in small bills, you've got a good bargain."

Her proposal is of course an unbelievable bargain, but Miguel decides not to accept immediately. "I'll need to call my bank," he says finally. After carefully inspecting the rugs once more. He says, "Do you mind if I step outside for a moment?"

A short distance from the door he calls his bank officer and arranges for additional funds to be available Monday morning in cash. Next, he calls his Santa Fe gallery director and tells him to catch the first flight to Roswell. This is the best buy he has ever made or will probably ever make. In fact he can hardly believe what is happening. "We have a deal," he tells Ms. Well a few minutes later. "I'll have the cash available for you Monday morning in small bills. Tomorrow I'll get some help, and with the Colonel's assistance, we'll select an interesting group of fifty pieces for your estate sale."

"Thank you, Mr. Jaramillo." replies Ms. Well. "It's been a pleasure meeting you."

"I assume you want a cut?" Miguel asks the Colonel, after Ms. Well leaves them alone together.

"Ten percent will be fine," the older man offers. I'll meet you here at 7:00 a.m. and we'll get started."

"Fine," Miguel agrees. "I wouldn't mind buying a few other items, but we'll look at them tomorrow."

When they reach Miguel's van, and shake hands, the Colonel leans close. "Remember," he says in a low voice, "You owe me big time. OK?"

"Since you're also charging her your normal fee, you've had a pretty good day yourself." Miguel replies, with a grin.

"But, of course, you're right, I do owe you."

Miguel mulls over the events of the day, on his way back to his car. *It's been a great day. Yes, indeed, a great day.* The last sale of an Early First Phase Chief's Ute blanket, in the condition indicated on the tag he just viewed, was five years ago. The price paid was just over $500,000.00. It was a private sale and certainly not public knowledge, but Miguel knew the wealthy collector who purchased the rare weaving and was well acquainted with the dealer who sold it. There are so few examples of this, the most desirable of all Navajo weavings, that there is no question this is his greatest buy and can't help but wish his father could have been with him today.

Driving away from Ms. Well's home, he heads North on Main Street, which takes him past the New Mexico Military Institute. On a recent stop in Roswell, the President referred to the Institute as the West Point of the West. Watching the cadets in formation on the parade ground, he remembers his gallery manager Paul attended school there and received an excellent education. Miguel wonders if Paul will want to visit his old school when he comes to help with the purchase.

CHAPTER 6

Miguel's cell phone rings as he arrives back in his motel room. He flips it open and answers.

"*Buenõs Dias, Senõr*," Armida greets him.

"*Buenõs Dias, Dõna*. How are you this fine day?"

"I'm great," she replies excitedly. "I have some good news for you. When can we get together?"

"I'm in Roswell on a buying trip," he replies. "I'm afraid I'm tied up for a few days but I should be back in Albuquerque Tuesday."

"I've come to some interesting conclusions about the weaving sample," she offers. "I'd like to share them with you as soon as you return. Will you give me a call? Perhaps we can have lunch."

"What are your plans for the weekend?" Miguel asks, deciding to take a chance. "I bought most of the Well's Navajo weaving collection. If you feel like it, how about helping catalog it, as we pack it for shipment?" He thinks, perhaps it will make good bait. She must know about the collection and how important it is.

"You bought all the Well's weavings?" she exclaims. Two blankets in the Well's collection are my favorite transitionals. They were on loan to our museum for years. The estate asked for their return last month for the auction. Our museum is planning on sending down an officer to bid on a number of pieces. How did you get them? We were told the auction was weeks away."

Miguel can hear the excitement in her voice. "I purchased all but fifty pieces directly from the heir." he explains. "But I haven't begun to inspect the collection. I start at 7:00 a.m. tomorrow. If you can get away for the weekend, I really could use your help in identifying them. I believe there's an early flight. My director from the Santa Fe gallery is coming. I'd love to have you here. Armida you'd have a chance to see some beautiful pieces. One of the blankets is an Early First Phase Ute Chief's Pattern blanket."

"Oh, my God. A First Phase Ute? What kind of condition is it in?" "I haven't unrolled it," he tells her. "But the condition tag rates it as mint condition. I thought you might like to do the honors." *Now that should bring her down here!*

"Miguel, how could you buy it without unrolling it?"

"I took a chance you would join me," he says. *There was nothing he wanted more than to have her with him now.* "I was about to call you."

Miguel knows how important this is to both of them, since the Ute variation of an Early First Phase Chief's Pattern blanket reveals the essence of Navajo aesthetics. With its paradoxical harmony and aggressiveness of weaving it is the "Holy Grail" of Navajo collectors; only a few examples of the early period Ute are known to remain. Miguel waits for Armida to answer, almost sure that she will not be able to resist.

"How many pieces are in the collection?" she questions.

"I would estimate at least 200. The fifty I didn't buy will be offered to the public. I got the rest for my galleries." Again he waits. And waits.

"Okay. I'll come and bring my camera?"

"*Bueno.* Catch an early flight. I'll pick you up at the airport. Give me a call when you're confirmed."

"Will do. I'll bring along the information on your weaving. I think you will be pleased with what we've discovered. I'll call for reservations. This sounds like fun. Thanks."

Miguel was well aware of how tempting his offer would be, but he can hardly believe she's accepted. Her knowledge will be invaluable as she checks over his purchase. Of course, he has been born and raised around Navajo weavings, but Armida's company is more than he could have hoped for. When they first met, although he was familiar with her heritage, he knew very little about her.

Miguel once wrote an extra credit report on New Mexico's diverse ethnicity, at the suggestion of his high school teacher. His study of the old New Mexico Castilian Spanish-speaking families like the Valenzuelas had indicated they were desperately trying to keep their family bloodlines as pure as those of the beautiful thoroughbred horses they bred.

Northern New Mexico is often described as the least American of any region of the continental United States. One of the main reasons for this area's unique character is the number of Castilian Spanish people who live there.

These people trace their bloodline directly to Spain, not South America or Mexico. After meeting Armida, Miguel researched the Valenzuela family and verified that they were longtime residents of a region purported to have a high percentage of Castilian Spanish blood. There are many cultural characteristics, which distinguish them from those who only speak Spanish. Armida's and the Valenzuela family's blue eyes were certainly one of those characteristics. Very few people of Mexican descent have blue eyes, but this trait is fairly common among the Castilian Spanish whose forefathers came directly from Spain.

With the Valenzuelas there's not only a family fortune to maintain, but also the stewardship of one of the last large Spanish land grant properties left intact in Northern New Mexico. Their bloodline is one of the purest of these old inhabitants of the "Land of Enchantment." Carlos, like his father and grandfather, holds his land together with will and wile. The Valenzuelas arrived in this region almost 350 years ago. Their title to the land was granted by the Spanish Crown and later confirmed by the Mexican Republic. Typical of land grants, the boundaries of the Valenzuela's land were ambiguous and indefinite. When the treaty of Guadalupe Hidalgo was signed on July 4, 1848, the Valenzuela family became American citizens and their land given *bona fide* recognition. However, over the years the family has been forced to fight many legal battles to hold on to their vast acreage. Only in Carlos' time, have the true legal boundaries been firmly established. Thanks in good part to his shrewdness and skillful use of his political influence.

Miguel is certainly aware of the current social structure in northern New Mexico where in some areas there is still a typical social pyramid. At the top are the Castilian Spanish-speaking men, called *patrones*. Although few in number, these grandees in whose veins flowed the best blood of Castile, sometimes have a tendency to disdain so-called Mexicans or Latinos. In the middle were the Latinos like Miguel and immigrants. The Native American Indians and illegal Mexicans are at the bottom. The elite Castilian population takes great pride in their pedigrees and their language, which differs noticeably from Mexican. They claim comparing their Castilian Spanish to Mexican Spanish is like comparing American English to British English.

He, like his father before him, courts these wealthy elite and knows them well. As a Catholic, Miguel knows the profound influence of the Roman Catholic Church in northern New Mexico. This heavy influence of the church often dominates the thinking, attitude and values of these proud people. Cognizant of this, his father carefully schooled Miguel to always be respectful of the church's importance, yet at the same time, he was able to instill a sense of Latino pride in Miguel. To be successful in any kind of a relationship with Armida, he must be careful not to step outside the bounds of the church. He realizes this will be an uphill battle. Miguel feels he must approach Armida with patience and caution. She's certainly worth the effort, but he knows Carlos will be the key.

He's always had his share of women, but he finds Armida special and is surprised this Castilian widow stirs him so. But the truth is, she's doing just that. He can't stop thinking about her. Of course, numerous obstacles to any kind of a long-term relationship with the lady will have to be overcome, not the least of which is Carlos Valenzuela. Carlos will surely pose a serious problem because Armida is his only child. For her to become involved with a Latino, a commoner like Miguel, might well be a real disappointment to the old Spaniard.

Deciding to take a little nap before going out for something to eat, he's just dozed off when the motel phone rings. "Colonel Briggs here. Do you have any plans for supper?"

Rubbing rubs his eyes, he replies, "None. I was trying to catch a few winks."

"How about joining me? I'll pick you up about six. My treat."

Miguel's glad for the company. Momentous things seem to be happening to him and somehow he doesn't feel like being alone tonight.

"Good! See ya at six," replies Miguel.

Miguel takes out his laptop, plugs it into the phone jack, to check the Internet and finds a few e-mails, including one telling him that Paul will be arriving on the early flight. The use of the Internet is valuable to Miguel. Although he isn't sure if it's of any importance to his galleries, he's established a web site to test the market. He checks eBay regularly to see what Navajo weavings are being offered.

He's dressing when Armida calls to tell him her reservation is confirmed on the early flight. "I'll meet your plane." he tells her.

When the Colonel arrives to pick up Miguel, he says. "If you don't mind, I'd like to go to Artesia. It's a short drive and there's a restaurant there I think you'll enjoy, OK?"

When they are on the road, Miguel asks. "How was your day?"

"Good. But I have to admit I was amazed by your transaction with Mrs. Well. I don't handle a large number of Navajo rug deals at my auctions, I usually do farm sales and I've never seen anything quite like what happened today. Mrs. Well bumped you $50,000.00 and you never blinked an eye. You easily popped for $150,000.00. What the hell is so special about old Navajo rugs? Is there really that much interest in them?"

Miguel offers, "Navajo blankets and rugs have been collected for more than two hundred years." It always amazes him that people like the Colonel who live in the West can be so naive about the significance of something as desirable as Indian arts and crafts. "Navajo blankets are important cultural symbols, not only among the Navajos but also among many native Americans, especially the Plains Indians. Starting in the 1840s, early explorers, followed by American soldiers, and government agents and then American tourists who traveled into the Southwest bought Navajo Blankets for souvenirs," Miguel adds.

"I didn't realize they were still that popular."

"You bet. Even artists collect Navajo blankets and rugs because of their strong visual statement." Miguel says, trying not to sound too pedantic. "Navajo textiles are outstanding examples of both historic and contemporary primitive art. Art collectors value them highly, not only for the beauty of these weavings but also for their investment potential, which has risen sharply in recent years."

"But aren't they still weaving?"

"Yes. But the number of weavers continues to decline every year. And because of the diversity of the regional styles and the superb technical aspects of modern weaving, the best contemporary rugs are collected as avidly as are the fine Classic, Late Classic and the colorful Transitional Period textiles."

"I see. But what makes the Well's collection so special?"

Miguel debates silently a few moments, then decides he owes the Colonel an explanation. After all it's the Colonel's invitation that has given him the opportunity to make the buy of his life.

He begins by explaining that for the most part, the weavings in the collection are not really rugs. Most of them are wearing blankets. Not only wearing blankets but very old, very special, blankets. Navajo weavers never wove rugs until the white man came. They would sometimes sit on their blankets but never used them as rugs. However, in the late 1800's the operators of Indian trading posts encouraged them to weave rugs. Navajos were being supplied with machine-made blankets, primarily Pendleton wool blankets, causing the weaving of fine blankets for their own use to virtually stop. For a short time, they continued to produce a few blankets for trade. However, after the traders encouraged them to go into the production of rugs, by 1910 the fine light blankets were a thing of the past.

"I'm sure you know what you are doing," the Colonel tells him. "But it seems like a lot of money to put out with a casual walk past those racks. Have you got reliable help coming?"

"Yes, my gallery director and the head curator from the Taylor Museum in Albuquerque are flying in tomorrow morning. I'll pick them up, get them checked in, and we'll be over to the house."

The dinner in Artesia is excellent. The La Fonda restaurant is everything the Colonel promised. The food is authentic New Mexico cuisine featured on a buffet that includes Chiles Rellenos, stuffed Chimichangas, Corn Chowder Con Questa, New Mexican style Veal Parmesan and an assortment of appetizers, salads and side dishes.

At the Colonel's request, during dinner, Miguel continues his narrative about the collection. Explaining that some of the rugs in the collection are "Pound Rugs" and indicates these should be included in the ones for the Colonel's auction. Pound rugs are colorful; they were woven at the height of the Trading Post era sometimes referred to as the transitional period, a time when the trading post owners were buying the rugs by the pound. The Indians soon caught on, and often brought in coarse rugs made from poorly cleaned and carded wool. They even went so far as to pound sand into the uncleaned wool to increase the rug weight. There were also a number of other rugs in the collection woven during this same period.

Miguel indicates that the other weavings in the Well's collection are for the most part pre-nineteen hundred weavings. Many of which represent the Classic period of weaving, when the weavers used bayeta; a wool cloth manufactured in England and supplied to the Navajos by the Spanish and a group of newly arrived Hebrew merchants. Mr. Well also accumulated a number of finely woven pieces made with Germantown yarn. Blankets from this expensive Pennsylvania yarn are some of the most desirable weavings as the crafty trading post operators carefully distributed the yarn only to the best weavers.

The rest of their dinner conversation covers some other items Miguel is interested in. Of particular interest to Miguel are several Apache woven baskets and a Kiowa Ghost dance shirt. They decide to look at those in the morning when the Colonel admitted that there is another buyer scheduled to look at them Monday morning.

As they reach the outskirts of Roswell on their return, Miguel is surprised when a Stealth fighter plane, engaged in touch and go landing practice at the old Airport, flies low over them. Pulling to the side of the road, they watch as the weird craft circles and returns to again fly close over them toward the old airbase, once known as Walker Airfield. The jet-black Stealths' triangular shape is eerie, almost like something from outer space. The Colonel explains that the Stealth Squadron at Holloman uses the field regularly for practice landings. because there is so little air traffic here in Roswell, The airfield is now used primarily for airplane storage, painting and restoration.

Back in his motel room, Miguel is almost too excited to fall asleep, not only about the purchase he's about to make, but also the fact that Armida has agreed to come and assist him. Tomorrow will be one of the most important days of his life and Armida will be there to share it with him. How could anything go wrong?

CHAPTER 7

Jacinto Reyes's instructions to Armando are crystal clear.

"Get the damn weaving back from the Valenzuela woman."

It's obvious he isn't about to accept any excuses and couldn't care less how Armando gets it done. His voice rises.

"Do you understand? Damn it! Get it back."

To be sure, Armando is no saint. In his time he's done it all. But this is risky, very risky. Particularly because the Reyes brothers want him to work outside his agency.

Armando looks across the table at Jacinto Reyes. Sitting in the coffee shop on the airport concourse, this is the first time they've met. Jacinto is a big, muscular, hawk-faced man with dark brooding eyes, and tattoos on both hands. In his business Armando learned early on to read people pretty well and he recognizes the type. This man is someone you don't want to ransom, but Armando's no amateur; he thinks it might be worth a go. His telephone calls to this character's brother, Tomas, have indicated they are well heeled and Armando's not shy about charging for his services. Jacinto takes a long, slow look at him.

"We'll pay $1,000.00 to get the sample back."

Sitting back in his chair, Armando mulls it over before deciding to try for a bump. "Make it $2,000.00 and you've got a deal. Half now, the balance on delivery."

The look in Jacinto's eyes tells him he may have made a mistake. But after a long silence, Jacinto takes out his wallet and counts out ten one hundred-dollar bills. Leaning across the table, he hands them and his card to Armando. In a low growl, Jacinto says, "Here's the $1,000.00. Get it done and bring it to me. But don't fuck with me. Understand?"

Armando offers, "Relax, I've done this kind of work before. I'll get it."

"You better damn well do it and soon. Call me." Then Jacinto closes his briefcase, gets up from the table, and tosses a five-dollar bill at the check and snarls, "This should cover it." He roughly pushes his way past a young couple, who look at him in surprise before he disappears through the coffee shop door.

Running his hands through his hair, Armando thinks, what the hell have I got myself into? I'm way to old for this shit. But he has never walked away from a job once started, and he isn't about to do it now. A leopard doesn't change his spots.

***

The Taylor Museum at the University of New Mexico is far from a secure facility and with very little effort, Armando finds out where Armida

Valenzuela's office is located. With his back pain deadened by drugs, Armando enters the office complex of the museum late in the afternoon, posing as a city building inspector. On the second floor, where Armida's office is located, he simply slips into a utility closet and waits.

After two hours, when all is quiet, he opens the door a crack. He listens for any activity, but hears none. The floor's empty and there appears to be no one left in this part of the building. Cautiously, he makes his way to Armida's office, the second door on the left. Placing his ear to the door he listens, then tries it, discovering to his surprise that it isn't locked. Opening the door, he slips inside and goes directly to the file cabinets on his right.

Probing through all four cabinets, one by one, he finds no sign of the plastic envelope or the weaving scrap. He's jimmying open the desk and rummaging through it when he hears a door open down the hallway and two people talking. Ducking down behind the desk, he waits nervously as they move down the hallway past the office. He struggles to slow his heartbeat. When all is again quiet, he methodically continues his search through Armida's desk and is about to open the last drawer when something stops him. Looking up, he sees a young woman wearing a white lab coat staring at him.

"What are you doing in here?" Mary Chaves demands in a shrill voice.

Without hesitating, Armando moves around the desk and charges her. For a gimpy, old man, he's surprisingly quick and Mary is completely taken by surprise as he roughly pushes both hands into her chest. Caught offguard, unable to maintain her balance, Mary falls backward, striking her head on a protruding door jam. Armando forgets all about his search for the weaving and exits the building as fast as he can.

It's nearly ten minutes before the cleaning crew arrives to find Mary. She's unconscious and has lost a large amount of blood. Realizing she's badly injured, the cleaning supervisor calls 911.

Armando is long gone by the time the ambulance arrives to transport Mary to the hospital.

Later, when he arrives home, Armando reports his failure to find the weaving.

"You bumbling idiot," Jacento screams into his phone, clearly furious. "What the hell went wrong?"

"Relax. I'll find it." Armando tells him with more confidence that he feels. "She must have done something with it. I'm sure she still has it. I'll find it. I just need a little more time."

Jacinto is in no mood for delays. He knows the longer the weaving is out of his hands the sooner he and Tomas will find themselves in hot water. "Maybe she gave it back to the trader." He offers.

"No. I don't think so," replies Armando. "I understand he's out of town, on a buying trip. I don't believe he's seen her since he gave her the damned thing."

"Well, earn your money. God Damn it. Ffffiiind it."

Armando hears the phone disconnect and begins to sweat. He knows he shouldn't have taken this job. Now there's a witness to deal with, the woman who discovered him in Armida's office and he wore no disguise. What happens if the woman identifies me? How in the hell have I gotten myself into this mess? He heard the thud as her head hit the door jam but he has no idea how badly she's hurt. His pain pills have worn off and his back's killing him. He knows he needs to take a look in Armida's apartment. Maybe the weaving scrap is there. First, however, he needs a little rest. Taking two of his pain pills he sets his alarm clock. Sitting on the side his bed, he contemplates his fate. Finally his pain subsides, and he lays down across his bed and falls into a fitful sleep.

CHAPTER 8
Roswell New Mexico

Miguel watches as the little turboprop plane touches ground on time and taxis up. He waits for Paul Aragon, his gallery director, and Armida to exit the plane. They're both carrying luggage and chatting as they move toward him. After greeting them, he takes Armida's carry-on luggage from her.

"I see you two have met," he says, "How was your flight?"

Armida, dressed in a moss print broomstick skirt and a black crinkle rayon top, is breathtaking. "Delightful." She replies, her eyes sparkling. "The air was crystal clear and we could see from horizon to horizon. There was a still a little snow left on the Capitan Mountains and they were a beautiful sight from the plane."

"How about some breakfast?" Miguel asks. As they walk toward his car, trying to stay calm at Armida's nearness.

"We've got a long day ahead of us. I've got your room keys. You both can freshen up, change into your work clothes, and then we'll get a bite to eat. The motel offers a good-looking breakfast menu."

Miguel calls the auctioneer from the lobby, and tells him they will be a little late. He's glancing at the local morning newspaper when Armida comes in. She's changed into a pair of tan jeans and a bright red sweatshirt sporting a New Mexico Lobo logo. She has a photographer's carrying case slung over her shoulder, Paul is following close behind.

Breakfast in the motel restaurant is leisurely as Paul and Armida continue to become acquainted. Miguel finds he can't keep his eyes off of Armida who's telling Paul about her trip to the Phelps Museum where he once spent a summer as an intern. She's animated and vibrant as they compare notes about the museum's director and extensive collection. As he watches her he finds himself once again aroused.

An hour later, Miguel introduces Armida and Paul to Colonel Briggs who takes them directly to the carriage house and leaves them to their business. Miguel finds the Well's inventory information stored in a professionally organized set of files in a cabinet. Upon inspection, Miguel discovers what appears to be an individual file folder for each weaving.

Every weaving is numbered and the corresponding file folder has the acquisition information and provenance recorded in it. Miguel asks Armida to take a look and after reviewing a stack of the folders, she randomly selects three folders and asks to see the corresponding weavings. Paul and Miguel search the racks and pull the three weavings she has selected.

Armida spreads them out on the tables in the center of the room and begins to compare them to the information in the file. Miguel watches quietly as she meticulously goes over the weavings and makes her comparisons.

Fifteen minutes later she announces, "I don't know who did this catalog work, but it's the work of a professional. These records are exceptional. Who ever did these really knew their stuff. I'd like to pull a few more samples, and if they're comparable to these, I'd say you can rely on all the information contained in these files. The only problem I see is the photos. Quite a few of them are poor quality Polaroids."

Miguel replies, "That's great news, if we can utilize the files, it'll save a lot of time."

The second batch of files checks out the same as the first three, so Miguel decides to use the records to do a preliminary search for the fifty rugs he's agreed to leave for the auction.

Sorting out a batch of files for inspection takes a half-hour. Then Paul pulls the weavings. Each weaving is carefully rolled in a protective white cotton sheet and he brings them to the tables for inspection. Armida and Miguel wear cotton gloves and check each piece, Miguel occasionally asking her opinion.

Finally, when they take a break, Armida gives Miguel a bright smile. "When do I get to see the good stuff?" She asks.

"Where's that First Phase Ute?"

Miguel offers, "Next to the last rack, Paul, would you get it for the lady?"

Wearing a fresh pair of white cotton gloves, Armida removes the protective covering.
As she slowly and carefully unrolls the old blanket, the alternating bands of white and natural dark brown, lined with wide bands of Indigo blue strips become visible.

Miguel knows she's aware that this variation of the Chiefs Pattern does not contain any of the narrow Bayeta marking strips used in other First Phase Pattern blankets.

Most experts believe Navajo weavers produced these beautiful wearing blankets as trade goods for their Ute neighbors to the North. The Utes showed a preference for the indigo blue and a special fondness for this particular pattern. They're looking at the rarest of all Navajo blankets and Miguel can no longer resist. He must get his hands on it.

Donning new gloves, he inspects the Indigo threads to assure himself they are not made of Bayeta wool. Satisfied, he carefully inspects the weaving with his eyepiece.

For ten minutes Armida and Miguel, trying not to get in each other's way, inspect the blanket. It's constructed from the soft, handspun fine long fibers of the Merino sheep's back. Miguel notes approximately 80 warps per inch and the blanket was woven with a relatively wide weft size but still tightly warped, tighter than anything he has seen recently. Miguel's convinced he is looking at one of the finest Chiefs blanket ever.

"Well, what do you think of it?" Miguel asks.

Armida continues to gaze at the blanket speechless for a moment. She knows of no other example comparable to this weaving. Its condition is superior. There's no evidence of moth damage and it is in mint condition.

"It's beautiful," she answers in a quiet voice. "One of the nicest blankets I've ever had my hands on. Our museum would love to have it. We've looked for a First Phase Ute for years. I saw one in Denver while I was working on my grant, but it wasn't in this condition." Armida's face is flushed and her hands tremble slightly as she once again bends to inspect the warp of the blanket. She smiles and her voice lowers. "This is a beautiful, artistic, highly desirable weaving. Did you notice the looser weave that creates a softer, more clinging type of blanket? I love the deep, rich blue, and the obvious care with which the weaver chose to use only the long fibers from the sheep's back."

When they return it to the rack, they hear Paul exclaim.

"My god, there's another one here!"

"What?" Not another Ute?" exclaims Miguel.

Armida and Miguel both rush to the rack where Paul is pulling out another weaving.

"The tag only says Chief's Burial Blanket #627," he tells them. "But you can see through the sheet. It's a Ute."

Miguel is so stunned that it takes him a moment to get a grip on himself.

"Paul," he says, "get it out of there. Let's have a look."

Armida goes to the cabinet and removes the file #627. Opening the folder, she finds a letter and a photograph of a dead Indian, his head obviously scalped, propped up against a rock outcropping. He's wearing what could be a First Phase Pattern blanket. Although the photo is black and white, on the right side of the blanket she sees what appears to be a dark stain, which might be blood from a gunshot. In the photo, an army officer stands next to the body of the Indian proudly holding an old Sharp rifle. She's just begun to read the faded copperplate script when Miguel calls to her to come over to the table. There, fully unrolled, is a dirty old blanket. It's a First Phase, but not a Ute variation, and it's in rough shape. Closer inspection discloses a large dark stain around a hole; Armida realizes it could be the blanket draped around the body of the old Indian in the photo. Handing the photo to Miguel, she bends down and begins to closely examine the blanket.

"Well, what do you think?" asks Armida, continuing her examination.

"What else is in the file?" Miguel replies.

"Only an old letter." She hands him the letter and continues to examine the blanket. It's well worn and obviously in its found condition. The narrowness of the blue stripes and the fine red bands separating them from the white and dark brown strips indicate an early First Phase but not the Ute type. Closer inspection confirms her suspicion as she notices that the red bands are made from rewoven Bayeta wool.

"Did you read this?" Miguel asks her in a stunned voice.

"No, I didn't get a chance. What is it?"

Armida is standing close to Miguel and she moves closer to get a better view of the old letter as Miguel continues.

"It appears to be provenance stating this blanket was worn by Narbona when he was killed," he tells her. "The man with the gun in the photo is Colonel James Macrae Washington, military commander and governor of the Territory of New Mexico in 1849. The photo was taken at the Canyon de Chelly site when Narbona was shot during a dispute over a stolen horse. It's coming back to me now. Narbona was a famous leader of the Navajos and his death a major loss for the Navajo Nation. A loss that started a bloody war between the Indians and the Territorial forces. Old man Well must have obtained the blanket from an heir of the Colonel."

"My God. What a find," Armida gasps. "The story of the Colonel and his botched negotiations with the Navajos is a historical gold mine. Do you have any idea the significance of this piece?"

"I have a feeling you're going to tell me!" Miguel says with a sly grin.

"You bet I am," she counters. "I'm warming up right now, and you're going to have a devil of a time holding on to this."

And at that moment, Miguel realizes that Armida is clearly as serious as a heartbeat and her presence here might be a serious mistake. The public notoriety over the discovery of an item of this historical importance could cause him problems, something he doesn't need. He prefers a low profile, particularly in view of the buy he is making on this cache of weavings. "Armida," he says, making a quick decision, "suppose you take the blanket to the museum and do the historical work. All things considered, I think Mr. Well did the right thing by keeping it in a found condition. All I ask is to retain title and be anonymous until I make a decision to donate it. Fair enough?"

Delighted, Armida agrees to his terms. Folding the old blanket into a manageable size, she places it in a plastic garbage bag she can carry on the plane. They return to the work of sorting, almost too excited to concentrate. When they have selected the fifty weavings for the auction, Miguel suggests they break for lunch.

It's nearly 2:00 p.m. when Armida's cell phone rings. Her eyes grow wide and before Miguel can register that something dramatic has happened, she throws herself into his arms.

"Someone broke into my office and hurt my friend Mary." she cries as he holds her close. Then getting a little better grip on herself she continues. "She's in the hospital. I've got to get back to Albuquerque."

"Do they know how badly she's hurt?" Miguel asks, drawing her back into his arms.

"They say she has a concussion and there might be serious brain damage," Armida continues with a sob. "They may not know how bad she is for a couple of days. I don't understand why anyone would break in and ransack my office? I don't have anything of value there."

"I'll find out when the next flight leaves for Albuquerque," Miguel says. "I'll take you out to the airport, if you like." Armida wipes away her tears. "Thank you. I'm a mess. Take me back to my room and I'll get ready to go."

Miguel makes a reservation for her on the next available flight. Sitting on the edge of his motel bed, he recalls holding Armida in his arms, her warm breasts pressing against him, and thinks about how very special she is. Not only do they share a common interest in Navajo weaving but they both love New Mexico and it's long history.

Picking up the phone, he calls her room. Fifteen minutes later, they check her out of the motel and are on their way to the airport. "We haven't discussed your weaving sample." Armida reminds him.

"Here's what Mary and I discovered." As she relates the information on the scarp, she seems calm and collected. The perfect professional again, but Miguel can tell she's worried. And that's understandable. She must feel responsible to some degree for what has happened in her office even though she has no idea why Mary was attacked. Only when they're grabbing a quick bite to eat at the airport restaurant, does she ask Miguel where the scrap came from, and even then was so clearly distracted that she barely listens to his explanation.

Standing at the gate, just when he is about to tell her how much he appreciates her coming, she suddenly steps up, presses herself against him and offers her mouth. Miguel bends down and they kiss. For a brief moment they are both lost in each other. It feels right.

Armida lightly touches his face, brushing it softly with her fingers. "I've got to go," she says. "Thanks." Turning away she moves quickly toward the runway apron.

Moments later, watching her plane taxi down the runway; Miguel can't help but wonder what he is sending her back to. The best he can do is hope that what ever is going on will not endanger her. With no clue why her office has been broken into, he doesn't know what to do to assist her. He only knows he needs to wrap up his business here and get back to Albuquerque as soon as possible, where he can be with her. For the first time, he realizes how deeply he cares for her. His new found feelings surprise him but at the same time are exciting. This lady is definitely complicating his life. *I'm in love,* he thinks to himself.

CHAPTER 9

Armida finally convinces the Morrison Hospital staff of her close relationship to Mary and is allowed into the I.C.U. to see her. She's taken to Mary's curtained bed and is instructed she can only stay for ten minutes. Mary's head is heavily bandaged and a nurse is bending over her, checking one of the leads to the heart monitoring system.

Squeezing back a tear she approaches Mary's bed and takes her hand. Overcome at seeing Mary lying there, so pale and still, she gathers up her courage to ask the nurse about Mary's condition. "How's she doing?" Does she even know I'm here?"

"I really don't know, I just came on duty." the nurse tells her. I understand she hasn't regained consciousness since they brought her in. I believe she's scheduled for surgery in the morning. Perhaps you should speak with the supervisor. She can tell you more."

Armida stays a few more minutes then goes to the nurse's station and asks to speak with the supervisor. When she arrives, Armida introduces herself, explaining her relationship to Mary. The supervisor is relieved to see Armida. "We have your friend scheduled for surgery and I need a signature from one of her next of kin."

Armida tells her Mary's parents and husband were deceased and she knows of no other relatives in the United States, other than Mary's six year old son Jessie. The supervisor says Mary's surgery is exploratory but very serious. The X-rays show what appear to be blood clots on Mary's brain, and some swelling. Either one of these problems could be life threatening.

Armida agrees to furnish Mary's insurance information for the hospital and is allowed to sign forms that grant permission for the surgery. Since Mary is sedated and there's nothing she can do for her, Armida decides to go home.

Using her cell phone she calls Stacy, Mary's roommate, and is relieved to hear Stacy will be able to take care of Jessie as long as necessary.

Armida's condo is twenty minutes away from the hospital. She takes out her door key but to her surprise finds the door is unlocked. Opening it cautiously, she freezes as she sees her living room looks like a hurricane has swept though it. Drawers are pulled out and dumped, furniture is overturned and pictures pulled from the walls and taken out of their frames. Shards of glass are scattered everywhere on the floor. Armida is so shocked she simply stands there for a few moments stunned. With her heart pounding in her chest she checks the other rooms, only to find them in similar condition.

She calls the police and while she waits for them to arrive, attempts to determine what has been taken. The obvious things like her CD collection, stereo, and television are untouched and in the bedroom, although her clothes are strewn everywhere and her bed sheets are on the floor. Her extensive collection of Indian jewelry is intact.

For an hour the policemen and their CID crew, meticulously go though each room. They question Armida, but she is unable to give them any idea who might be responsible for this or her office break-in. When they finally leave, Armida straightens out her bedroom, takes a shower and gets ready for bed. She decides to wait until the morning to call her father. She bought her condo near the college after selling the home she and Jose had shared. She doesn't want her father again telling her how she should live in a more secure area. She simply wants to get some sleep.

Lying in bed, no matter what explanation she tries to come up with, there seems to be no rationale for her office and condo being ransacked. After exhausting every possible reason, to no avail, a weary Armida finally falls asleep.

***

In Roswell, the next morning, after a few intense discussions, Miguel and the Colonel finally agree on a price for the pots and other Plains Indian artifacts Miguel has selected and he approves the list of 50 rugs to be in the auction. Finally, with negotiations over, the Colonel leaves for the main house to consult with Mrs. Well. While Paul, with the help of one of the Colonel's people, continues sorting and loading the rental truck.

Miguel has selected very superior artifacts, consisting of a Cheyenne Pictorial Cradle circa 1880, a Kiowa Ghost Dance Shirt circa 1880-1890, a Plains painted hide war shield and cover, several pieces of San Ildefonso black/Reyes pottery, and a Margaret Tafoya Santa Clara blackware pottery jar. To round out the group, he also has selected four Apache baskets bringing the negotiated price to $28,000.00, plus the 10% commission for Colonel Briggs. The total matches Miguel's cash reserve limit. It has been a great weekend except for news of the attack on Armida's friend. Miguel decides to let Armida contact him, rather that trying to phone her. He knows she will have a full plate with her friend in the hospital and the inevitable police inquiry that is bound to follow the break-in of her office.

Grace Well has just finished approving the inventory of weavings he and the Colonel selected for the auction and they are firming up the prices on the balance of his purchase when Armida calls. He can tell immediately she is very upset.

"Miguel, Mary is going to have surgery this morning." Armida tells him, her voice edged with anxiety. "She's not doing well. They say she has some swelling in her brain. I'm so worried and when I got home last night, my condo had been ransacked. I don't understand what's going on or who's doing all this. I don't have anything anybody would want. Now I have to go down to the police station."

Miguel exclaims, "My God. I'm so sorry. I hope Mary will be all right. I have to be at the bank when it opens up in the morning, but I'll come to Albuquerque as soon as I settle up. Have you called your father?"

"Yes, he's on his way here. Miguel, Mary has a little boy Jessie and she has no relatives here in the states. I've just talked to Papa and he's going to take Jessie back to the hacienda."

"Do the police have any idea who is behind all this?"

"I don't know. The people who were here last night left without saying anything. Maybe I'll find out something at the police station. Miguel, I don't mean to bother you with all this, I wanted you to know."

"Don't be silly. I'm so sorry I can't be there today. I'll have my gallery director in Albuquerque give you a hand. Let me give you his cell phone number."

"No. I'll be all right." she assures him. "Papa will be here soon and I can manage."

"Please let me know if there is anything I can do, and I'll call you first thing when I get there."

"I will. I'm sorry to trouble you."

"Look, take care of yourself Armida. Look over your shoulder once in a while and keep your eyes open."

"Thanks." There is a soft breathiness to her voice Miguel hasn't heard before. It made his heart race.

After Armida hangs up, Miguel goes back to his negotiating, although it's difficult for him to concentrate. With the news of Armida's condo being ransacked he's beginning to have real concerns for her safety. And here he is in Roswell unable to be of any assistance.

It's almost noon when Mrs. Well finally accepts his offer for the thirteen additional selected items. Because it looks like Paul will be able to finish loading before the bank opens the next morning, she also agrees to let Paul head out for Santa Fe as soon he's finished.

Miguel reviews the inventory listing of his purchases, later that afternoon, back in his motel room, The weavings cover the entire Classic and Transitional period and even includes a few modern examples by superior weavers. Of course, the crown jewel is the Early First Phase Ute. His purchases also include serapes, ponchos, children's blankets, and eye-dazzlers. Completing his selection are a few wedge weaves, Second and Third Phase Chief's pattern blankets, far more than he bargained for when he made his first offer. With the Indian Market in Santa Fe a few weeks away, this is a most opportune purchase. His acquisition has been spectacular, the kind that would have made his father proud. But all he can think about is Armida and her problems and it mutes any feelings of satisfaction he has. He needs to be with her, as soon as possible.

CHAPTER 10
Albuquerque

Today is not a good day for the Albuquerque police department. Word has come down from Carlos Valenzuela to the Senate Majority leader, who in turn contacted the Mayor of Albuquerque, who contacted the Police Chief, who called Captain Juan Hernandez, who has assigned Detective J.T. Romero to solve the break-in of Armida's apartment and Mary's assault. Captain Hernandez is an old street cop who was at one time J.T.'s partner. He knows that J.T. can be trusted to handle a hot case like this one. Even though J.T. is a bit rusty he's politically astute, and Hernandez knows J.T. will keep him advised of the cases' progress. In New Mexico, when one of the most powerful Castilian men in the state cracks the whip, everyone hops to. As expected, J.T. drops everything to work exclusively on this case.

J.T. interviews the officers who responded to the 911 call from Armida's apartment and finds out that Armida has reported there appears to be nothing missing from her apartment. With little else to go on, the officers, who have a particularly heavy caseload, have put this investigation on the back burner.

J.T. is the senior detective in the Albuquerque, New Mexico Police Department, with only two years to go before his retirement, At this stage of his career, he has seen it all, but lately he seems to be having a string of bad luck. It's almost as if he has bad karma. After fighting a weight problem for twenty years, he's finally given up, his two hundred-pound body is the result. J.T.'s nickname is 'The Nose,' not only because he sports a hawk-like proboscis, but over the years, particularly his early years before DNA, he frequently found clues others had missed.

Now, as he contemplates his retirement, he realizes he's getting out at the right time. When the scientific boys show up at a crime scene, he's often forced to take a back seat while they do their thing. All too frequently, he finds himself in the humiliating position of being unable to touch anything or even look around until they finish their investigation. J.T.'s not a happy camper these days and is both surprised and flattered when he's suddenly handed a high priority case. Evidently the high-tech boys have stubbed their toes once too often. He realizes he might be past his prime but he recognizes a hot case when he sees one and this Valenzuela case is definitely hot if for no other reason than the victim's father is one of the most important men in the state.

Following his time honored technique, on foot; J.T. goes about the tedious task of interviewing all of Armida's neighbors, one by one. In his opinion, it's the best way to solve a case, the sure way. This time his break comes when he knocks on the door of an old brownstone across the street and one door west of Armida's condo. Looking at his identification, he's greeted by Mrs. Harris, a frail, white-haired elderly lady who tells him she might be able to help. She invites him in and seats him at a table, then scurries off to her kitchen to get him a cup of coffee.

Looking around the apartment, J.T. observes dozens of photos of babies, weddings, and family groups, as well as several photos of a handsome young man in an out-of-date police uniform. All the frames are old and many of the photos are faded with age as is everything else in the apartment. The one exception is a shiny new pair of high-powered binoculars, which sit on a little table beside a chair in front of a window.

Returning from the kitchen, Mrs. Harris has a plate of sugar cookies along with his cup of coffee and her tea.

"How long have you lived here?" J.T. asks.

"Oh my! Let's see? It must be thirty-eight, no thirty- nine years now."

"Do you live alone?"

For the next ten minutes he listens to her family history, a sad one to be sure, since she lost her husband in the Korean conflict and her son, a Los Angeles policeman, was killed about ten years later in a shoot out with a drug dealer. Now, her only family consists of a sister who lives in California. J.T. estimates she must be at least eighty years old. "You mentioned you might be able to help me," he prompts, cutting through the flow of words that threatens to never stop.

"I need to know if you saw anything unusual the day your neighbor Armida Valenzuela's condo was ransacked."

"Well, it was a cloudy day and I remember there was an old sedan parked across the street for over an hour that day."

"You didn't happen to notice the license plate did you?"

It was along shot, more than he could reasonably hope for, but he had to ask.

"No, but it had obviously been in a wreck, there was a large dent over the rear wheel on the driver's side and I saw the driver. He walked bent over and had a limp. He came out of the building and got into the parked car. He seemed like he was in a hurry, I knew he didn't belong there. When I heard about the break-in, I thought I should call someone, but Sam, the maintenance man in this building, told me he heard the pretty lady who lives there say nothing was missing so I didn't bother. Was there something missing?"

"No," J.T. told her. Looking out the window he realizes she probably had a clear view of the car and the intruder. "But we think there could be a connection between this break-in and another one where a woman was badly hurt. Hasn't anyone questioned you about this?"

"No. No one came to my house."

"Mrs. Harris, how many doors did the car have and what color was it?"

"I'm sure it had four doors and I think it was black, but it was so dirty I couldn't say for sure."

Mrs. Harris was now visibly upset. Her eyes widened and she looked as if she was going to cry. "Oh, my goodness," she continues, "I'm so sorry. I should have called, shouldn't I? I knew that man didn't belong in her building. The pretty lady never has any male friends. She's a widow you know, a young woman with the cute little boy stops by and once in a while her handsome father. Lately, I think she's been out of town a lot." Mrs. Harris finally stops talking long enough to take a sip of her tea and J.T. asks,

"Would you recognize the man with a limp if you saw him again?"

"Well, of course. There's nothing wrong with my eyesight or my memory."

After listening to more of the neighborhood gossip, than he cares to hear, J.T. excuses himself, says good-by and heads for the University campus. It's clear to him there must be some connection between the two break-ins.

The notes given him by the campus police and the other investigating officers are little or no help. But J.T., not wanting to leave any stone unturned strikes up a conversation with the campus police. After gaining their total confidence, one of them finally mentions a log. Examining the entries for the day Mary was injured, he notices they issued several tickets for expired auto licenses.

New Mexico auto plates are updated using a small dated sticker applied to the plate in the lower right-hand corner to show the state fees have been paid. One of the campus tickets was issued the day of the office break-in to a 1985 four-door sedan for having an expired license plate. The log indicates it was parked for a long time in front of the very building where the lab assistant was found unconscious in Armida Valenzuela's office.

Back at headquarters, a trace on the plate ticketed by the campus police yields an interesting name, Armando Peralta. Armando's been a thorn in J.T.'s side for many years, in fact several years back he tried his best to put Armando away for breaking and entering the office of a local trucking company executive involved in a labor dispute. J.T. wasn't able to get a conviction but he was sure the old shamus had done the job. However, since Armando's accident, J.T. has lost track of the old detective. If Armando is involved in this affair there are plenty of reasons to dig deeper. Particularly since, for years, the old private investigator has been known to operate just on the edge of legality. He's been a suspect in several assaults, but never charged. J.T. was under the impression that Armando had retired, but now, it seems the shady old bastard is back at work.

Armed with Armando's address, J.T. goes to his home. The house is a low, one story flat roofed stucco, typical of many Albuquerque track homes that were being built right after World War II. The house and yard are in pitiful shape and badly in need of repair. A dirty 1985 black Ford, four-door sedan with a dent over the rear wheel well is parked in the driveway.

Armando is fixing his lunch when the doorbell rings. If he's surprised to see his old enemy standing on the doorstep, he doesn't show it.

"Have you got a minute? I think we have something to discuss." Says J.T.

"You better advise me of my rights," Armando grumbles as he limps his way back into the kitchen, J.T. close on his heels. "I'm too old for this shit. I'll fill in the holes for you, but I need some assurance you'll take it easy on me or it's no go."

J.T. never dreamed it would be this simple.

"Then you know why I'm here, don't you?" he asks. "Here's the deal." J.T. says not waiting for Armando to answer. "If you plead to simple assault, I'll see what I can do about the breaking and entering. Since nothing's missing, the DA might buy it. But it'll probably cost you your license this time. I can't guarantee anything."

"How do you take your coffee?" Asks Armando in a defeated voice.

"Black is fine," replies J.T.

Armando motions for them to sit at a small kitchen table piled with dirty dishes, magazines and newspapers

"I read about that woman in the paper. I didn't mean to hurt her. I was looking for something when she came in and I pushed her aside when I ran out of the room. I guess she fell. I didn't look back."

"What in the hell were you doing in Ms. Valenzuela's office?"

"What do ya think? I was hired to find something for a client."

"Who hired you?"

"A couple of guys. They hired me to trail a trader and place an envelope in his van, up in Crownpoint. It had a scrap of some old rug in it. The trader was supposed to look at it and give it back. But he gave it to the gal at the university instead. My clients panicked and wanted it back."

"Why did you try to steal it back? Why didn't you simply ask for its return?"

"These guys are a little shady. They have a reputation for getting what they want. My job was to tail the trader and report back. When I told them the trader passed the package onto the curator, my clients really came unwound. I was not about to cross a couple of characters like them. I did what they wanted. That's all I know."

Without raising his voice, J.T. reminded him of the deal.

"Ok, I want all the details," Peralta "and you damn well better not leave anything out."

CHAPTER 11

At the hospital Armida waits for word about Mary's surgery. Earlier, Carlos went down to the hospital cafeteria for a bite to eat. Now, twenty minutes later, the doctor comes in to the waiting room.

"Ms. Valenzuela?"

Armida rises and looking expectantly at the surgeon.

"Yes."

He smiles broadly and takes both of her hands. "I have good news for you. The surgery went very well. Our patient is in recovery and her vitals are excellent. She should recover nicely." Releasing her hands, he says.

"She's a very lucky young woman. You can visit her when she's out of recovery. But she needs her rest, so please make it brief."

Armida thanks the surgeon, warmly, then hurries down to the cafeteria to find her father.

***

Detective J, T. Romero, a large man gone soft, is a little out of breath after climbing laboriously up the stairs to Miguel's office. He takes a seat opposite Miguel and refuses an offer of coffee. "I need to ask you a few questions. I understand you're acquainted with Professor Armida Valenzuela."

"Yes, she's a friend." Miguel answers. "Is she all right?"

J.T. never answers a question directly if he can help it. In his opinion it's always better to let a suspect talk. He isn't sure of Miguel's connection to the case.

"Were you aware that both the Professor's office and her condo were broken into?"

"Yes Ms. Valenzuela called me when I was in Roswell." Miguel answers and again asks. "Is the professor all right?"

"She's fine, just shaken a bit."

"Professor Valenzuela was with me in Roswell when her assistant was injured. How is the young woman? I believe her name is Mary."

"She's out of surgery and will recover." J.T. tells him. "The man who attacked her is in custody. He claims his entry was an attempt to recover some material you gave Professor Valenzuela. A scrap of rug or blanket. What do you know about it?"

"I have no idea why anyone would do such a thing. Who is responsible for all of this?"

"A private investigator who claims he was hired to leave the item with you in Crownpoint, New Mexico. He said you gave it to Professor Valenzuela."

"Well, that part is correct." Miguel replies "I found the scrap on the seat of my van when I returned from an auction there a couple of weeks ago. It was in an envelope with a note scribbled on the front that read, 'We will be in contact.' It's a very old piece of Navajo wearing blanket. I gave it to Professor Valenzuela to examine and date.

"Do you have the envelope?" J.T. asks.

"No, I gave it to Professor Valenzuela. Have you asked her where it is?"

"I'm going to be talking to her next," the detective answers, heaving himself out of the chair. "I need the item as evidence because this is now a criminal case. I'll be in touch." And he leaves.

Miguel calls Armida's office, when he finds a minute and as soon as she answers the phone says.

"I tried your home."

"I'm so glad you've called," Armida replies and he can hear a little sob. "A detective just called. He's on his way over here. He's claiming the man responsible for attacking Mary is a private investigator, trying to find that piece of weaving you gave me."

"I know. He just left here. I don't have the slightest idea what the hell is going on. I'm so sorry I got you into this mess."

"Don't be silly. You couldn't have known. I'm just relieved Mary is all right. Did you find out who left the scrap with you?"

"No. If the detective knows, he isn't saying, but he did mention he needed it for evidence. Maybe he'll tell you.
By the way, I'd like to send Mary some flowers. Where is she?"

"How nice. She's in room 317 at Morrison Hospital." "When can I see you?" Miguel asks. Just hearing her voice triggers his emotions and once again he realizes how deeply he is beginning to care for her.

"Can we have dinner?"

"Perhaps later this week." Armida answers. There's too much going on, and I want to get Mary settled in at the ranchero. She's going to be staying there while she recovers. Give me a call. If I find out anything, I'll let you know."

"That's fine. I need to go to the Santa Fe Gallery. I'll be back tomorrow. Is there anything I can do for you?"

"No, I'll be OK. Things should settle down in a couple of days. Thanks for calling. Take care."

"Will do. Take care of yourself. You've got my card with my cell phone number. Please give me a call if you need anything."

"Bueno."

With his van loaded on I-25 driving toward Santa Fe, Miguels' thoughts turn to Armida. He's very concerned about her. Could it have been his fault that she's in this mess? It upsets him to think that he may have been the cause of any of her troubles. The more he is around Armida the more he wants to be with her. Now with the break-ins and Mary's injury he can't help but wonder if this will affect their relationship. Turning off I-25, he maneuvers in heavy traffic toward his gallery. He knows he is in love with Armida, but he must be realistic, their backgrounds could make it very difficult for him to ever have a serious relationship with her.

CHAPTER 12

J.T. Romero had listened without comment as Armando Peralta told his tale. The old detective was surprised that Armando had given up so easily and fingered Tomas and Jacinto Reyes as the pair who had hired him. Although he'd never personally had a run-in with the two Reyes brothers, like everyone in the department, he was certainly familiar with the two banditos.

Back at headquarters, the day after interviewing Miguel and Armida, J.T. pulls the jackets on the Reyes brothers. In some ways, they really are a fascinating pair. On three occasions Tomas and Jacinto were accused of selling fake antiques. In each case they had been able to come up with auction receipts proving they had unknowingly purchased the items in question as antiques. With no further proof of intent to defraud, the complaints had been dismissed. In another case, Tomas was also accused of writing a book, under an assumed name and for creating a nonexistent publishing house. The book featured hundreds of photos and histories of collectable brass belt buckles from the 1800's. Also included was information and photos of twenty so-called rare buckles made for famous companies like Wells Fargo, Winchester, Colt, and Pony Express. The scam was that Tomas had these particular so-called rare buckles produced and beautifully age-patinated by a bronze foundry in Taos New Mexico. The fake buckles cleverly featured the actual logos of the famous old companies.

When the book caught on collectors clamored for the *rare* buckles. Tomas and Jacinto made a couple of cross-county trips and sold the phony buckles at flea markets, antique stores and auctions. They had a sweet deal going until a writer for an antique magazine stumbled onto the scam by discovering the address of the publishing house was a vacant lot in Taos, New Mexico.

Although the writer could never prove Tomas was the author, he did effectively destroy the market for Tomas's book and his buckles in a series of magazine articles.

In another instance, the Reyes brothers were accused of hiring a redheaded whore and installing her in a trailer park across the street from a factory manufacturing limited edition plates for collectors. In a few weeks, she is said to have traded her wares for a large collection of plates sneaked out of the factory by horny men. Everything was going great until she contracted a venereal disease and passed it on to her customers in the plant. But, here again, the Reyes brothers were not prosecuted. They were also suspected of dealing in Indian artifacts obtained by grave robbing but again had not been prosecuted because of a lack of evidence.

J.T. is intrigued by the challenge. Perhaps its time these two were brought to justice and he is the man to do it. The last known address for Tomas Reyes is in the small community of Peralta located twenty miles south of Albuquerque along the Rio Grande River. Since J.T. is a good friend of the sheriff's deputy, Paul Aragon, who lives in Peralta, he calls and makes arrangements for Paul to be with him when he goes to Tomas's home.

Traveling south on I-25, J.T.'s drive takes him along the Rio Grande valley. At this time of the year the valley is in full bloom. The lush green, irrigated fields to his left stand in sharp contrast to the brown prairie land to his right. In some fields, neat rows of freshly cut alfalfa await a bailing machine. Here, the beautiful Rio Grande River courses long and deep through the heart of New Mexico.

He joins up with Paul in Peralta, and in Paul's cruiser they continue to travel south along the river to a newly manufactured mobile home, partially hidden from the road in a stand of tall trees. Pulling up in front, they catch a glimpse of a tall man, cell phone to his ear, who is clearing the top of an adobe wall in the back yard. Paul is sure it's Tomas, but neither he nor J.T. want to run down a fugitive in the thick Bosque along the river bottom. On their way back to the sheriff's station, Paul points out a man driving a red pickup.

"There's Jacinto, Tomas's brother," he says, then swings a U-turn and quickly overtakes Jacinto's pickup. When Jacinto spots the red lights and hears the siren, he pulls over to the side of the road to wait as Paul approaches on one side of the pickup and J.T. on the other.

Jacinto rolls down the window. "What can I do for you?" he demands, noticeably upset, his jaw tight and a frown on his face.

"Your license and registration," Paul barks.

"Is there a problem?" asks Jacinto now appearing to become a little nervous.

"Just hand 'em over," Paul says, holding out one hand.

After fumbling around in the glove compartment and his billfold, Jacinto finally locates them both and shoves them out of the window to Paul.

"Get out of the truck," Paul tells him.

"What's the problem?" Jacinto is now noticeably upset, his face is red and beads of sweat have popped out on his forehead.

"Get out of the damn truck," growls Paul.

Within a minute, Jacinto is standing with his legs spread and both his hands on the hood while Paul frisks him, placing Jacinto's billfold, cell phone, keys and some change on the hood of the pickup. Jacinto is cussing and objecting loudly.

"Where's Tomas?" J.T. asks.

"How the hell should I know? I was headed over to his place."

"We were there a few minutes ago and he wasn't home, maybe you can contact him by phone. He does have a cell phone doesn't he?" Paul asks.

"Good idea," said J.T., as he helps Paul stuff Jacinto into the back seat of Paul's cruiser.

"Why do you need to talk to him?" Jacinto asks them as Paul starts up the engine.

"We need to talk with both of you," J.T. replies. And it would be a lot better if you and Tomas were both here. If not, we'll have to take you in and issue a warrant for him. It's your call."

Less than a half-hour later, Thomas Reyes shows up at the sheriff's station, his attitude obviously indicating his displeasure at being there. J.T. and Deputy Sheriff Paul Aragon decide to question the two brothers separately, after agreeing Tomas seems to be the weaker of the two. Paul reads Tomas his rights in the interrogation room while J.T. paces back and forth.

"We already know you two are the ones who hired Armando Peralta," J.T. says when Paul is finished. "That makes you and Jacinto accomplices to an assault with attempt to do bodily harm, and a breaking and entering charge."

"Wait a minute." Tomas blurts out. "We had nothing to do with any assault or break-in. You can't pin crap like that on us."

"Don't be too damn sure. We have a full statement from Armando. He swears you two are the ones who hired him." J.T. bends over the desk, he looks straight into Tomas's eyes.

"You and your asshole of a brother are going down for this one," he threatens.

"Look, I told you, we had nothing to do with any break-in or assault," Tomas tells him helplessly. "Jacinto and I hired the old man to check on a rug dealer who has something belonging to us. It isn't our fault he broke-in and hurt somebody. I'm not saying another word without my attorney present."

"If that's the way, you want it. J.T. tells him. "I'll be happy to take you both back to Albuquerque for booking. I'm sure it will be interesting to see what a search warrant will turn up at you and your brothers' places. Maybe this time you won't get off so easy."

J.T. turns to Paul, "Keep him here while I talk with Jacinto."

"Not a problem," Paul replies.

In a room at the end of the hallway, J.T. advises Jacinto of his rights. "We have a full statement from Armando, your investigator." Bending down with his face right in Jacinto's, he says. "You're in big trouble buddy. This time it's not just bunco. It's assault with intent to kill and breaking and entering. You got anything to offer? Or do we take you and Tomas in and book you?"

"You got nothing. We never ordered any break-in or assault. You're bluffing. I want an attorney. Now."

"Okay, tough guy. A couple of detectives I work with have been aching to get a look inside you and your brother's operation. This should do it for them. It'll be interesting to see what they come up with. We'll get a search warrant while you and your attorney are getting your bail together. By the way, have you two dug any archaeological sites lately?"

"You two damn fools." J.T. continues. "The widow woman whose apartment and office you two paid the old man to break into is the only daughter of one of the most powerful men in the state. Do you have any idea how much shit this is going to get you? You've really stepped in it this time."

"Who's her Father?" Jacinto's voice quivering slightly.

"Carlos Valenzuela," J.T. tells him. "Do you recognize the name?"

It's clear that Jacinto knows damn well who Carlos is. "I need to talk with Tomas," he says, the bravado now missing from his voice.

In the office where Jacinto is being interviewed, J.T. and the deputy, after a brief discussion, allow the brothers back together."

"I'll give you five minutes," J.T. tells them. "Then, unless you two have something to say, we'll head for Albuquerque."

In the next room J.T. and Paul listens on a speakerphone as Tomas and Jacinto go at each other. Jacinto is furious, almost shouting.

"You should have found out who the hell that woman was before you sicced Armando on her. You damn fool. Look what you've got us into now."

"How was I supposed to know?" Whimpers Tomas.

"Didn't you recognize the name?" Jacinto growls.

"I don't keep up on political shit. That's your department."

"We better figure a way to get out of this," Jacinto warns him. "If they get a search warrant, you know what they're gonna find. I've got fresh dug pots all over my place, and you've got all the stuff we pulled out of the cave in Canyon de Muerto, including the rest of the old rug. If they find that stuff, the Feds and the Navajo council will be after our blood. Why in the hell didn't we sell the damn old blanket to that collector in Arizona? You had to get greedy."

"So I screwed up. Now what?" Pleads Tomas.

"I think the only thing we can do is come clean and take our chances. Maybe if we admit to hiring Armando, that crazy old detective will be satisfied. In the mean time, we can get rid of the pots and the rest of the stuff at your house. I think they're under the gun to solve the break-in and assault."

"Can we just say we didn't have no part in it?"

"They have to prove we did. That's the beauty of it.

"If you say so." Groans Tomas.

"When they come back, we'll do it!"

Driving back to Albuquerque after arranging for the brothers to be held while he gets a search warrant, J.T. is satisfied with his day's work. Because of Deputy Aragon and his clerk, J.T. have obtained signed statements from both Reyes brothers. He knows his chances of charging them, as accomplices to Armando's assault and break-in charges are slim, however he's sure there will be no problem getting a search warrant. He's confident a search of their homes will yield evidence of their nefarious activities. There's no question in his mind they are dealing in Indian artifacts illegally obtained by digging in forbidden land.

But the important thing is that at least now the Valenzuela family pressure will be off. With the old private investigator's confession and the Reyes brother's depositions, J.T. knows he can make the charges against the old investigator stick. With the charges against Armando and the Reyes brothers caught in some kind of illegal possession, surely the old *Padrone* will call off the dogs. What a great day. Yes, J.T. is pleased with himself. Turning on his radio he finds a country music station and lazily drives north on toward Albuquerque.

CHAPTER 13

Miguel can wait no longer. Two days have passed since he spoke to Armida, and he can't stop worrying about her. He calls her office.

"Good morning. Professor Valenzuela here. How can I help you?"

When he hears her sultry voice, Miguel feels a tremor in his soul, "*Buenõs Dias,* Armida. It's Miguel Jaramillo."

"*Buenõs Dias*, Miguel. I was just thinking about you!"

"How nice." Miguel tries to sound nonchalant. "How is your friend, Mary?"

"She's doing much better. I believe she's going to be okay. The doctor thinks there will be no further complications. He says she should be released Friday. I'm so relieved. They caught the guy who did it. The police detective was here and took the weaving sample as evidence and they said they would get it back as soon as possible. It's been such a mess."

"I'm so sorry," Miguel replies. "I know the scrap is valuable but who would have thought it could cause so much trouble. Look. I'm going to be back in Albuquerque today. If you feel up to it, how about having dinner tonight?"

"I've got a late staff meeting today. Perhaps tomorrow night?" Now that Mary is recovering nicely, she feels at ease, even a little excited, accepting his invitation. Since Miguel's kiss in Roswell, she's been unable to get this Latino out of her mind.

"Great, I'll cook. I fix a mean Fajita. My apartment is the third story of our Albuquerque gallery building. There's an entrance door on the right side of the gallery, just ring the buzzer. How about seven?"

"Fine, I'll bring the wine. One of our best."

"I look forward to seeing you! *Adios, Dõna.*"

"*Hasta la vista, Senõr.*"

Miguel is elated. He's taken two courses at Albuquerque's Southwest Culinary School, loves to cook, and this will give him a chance to show off.

On Friday afternoon Miguel, with a grocery list in hand, leaves the gallery early and stops by his favorite butcher. Together they select a beautiful piece of aged beef. A stop at a local grocery store completes his list and he hurries to his apartment.

***

In her tub, Armida is enjoying her bath. She prefers taking a bath rather than a shower. A long bath helps her relax. She sinks deep into the water and soaks restfully for ten minutes before getting out and toweling off. Going to her closet, she tries on several outfits, finally settling for a rose-colored, poet blouse and matching-tiered skirt. She accents the outfit with a silver and turquoise squash blossom necklace, several old Navajo bracelets, a couple of Zuni inlay rings and her new lizard boots. She knows Miguel will appreciate Santa Fe style dress and her Indian jewelry.

Applying a touch of eye shadow and mascara to accent her eyes and a light perfume, she brushes her hair and takes a final check in the mirror. Selecting a bottle of Valenzuela wine from a wine rack she hurries out to her BMW.

Meanwhile Miguel is in the kitchen and dinner is progressing nicely. Removing the strip steak from the marinade, he sets it aside and proceeds to prepare a tomatilla salsa, blue corn chips, a julienne cut jicama salad with warm sopaipillas and honey for dessert.

As someone who attends wine festivals each year and owns a nice selection, Miguel is looking forward to seeing what Armida's wine choice will be. As he prepares guacamole to accompany the fajitas, his mind drifts back to the day he visited the Valenzuela hacienda and how attractive Armida was as she strode toward him. Some women are pretty, some sexy, but few are elegant. Armida is definitely elegant with a walk and carriage that sets her apart, even in a crowd. She moves with ease and a sense of confidence. And no matter how she tries, she can't hide her femininity. Miguel has never known a woman of her age who is so completely enchanting, yet who in some ways seems vulnerable.

He's finishing the dressing for the salad when he hears the buzzer from below. Quickly washing his hands, he moves to buzz her up.

"Good Evening," Armida says, giving him a bright smile as she strides into the apartment and hands him the bottle of wine.

"Is there anything I can do to help?"

"How about trying some of your wine? The wine glasses are in the cupboard there."

The wine is a Ruby Cabernet with a fruity bouquet, which Miguel knows will compliment his fajitas nicely. After Miguel nods approvingly, Armida perches on a barstool at the breakfast-island and asks him where he learned to cook.

Miguel stops trimming the beef and answers. "I've taken a couple courses and in college my roommate's dad was a chef in Taos. He's the one who got me interested. The fajitas I'm preparing are one of his father's specialties."

As he explains more about his love of cooking, he senses Armida is genuinely interested in what he's saying. Watching her as she sits there on the high stool, Miguel can't help but notice how relaxed she seems, and yet how vulnerable she looks. Armida is poised, yet obviously at ease, her elbows on the bar, holding her wineglass in both hands, only occasionally taking a sip.

As for Armida, as she watches Miguel skillfully prepared their meal, she feels something stirring inside her. He wears a white dress shirt, open at the collar. Both sleeves are rolled up and she notices he wears no undershirt. His young body is well conditioned, and she enjoys watching him move about the kitchen so at ease.

At a beautiful mahogany table in a comfortable dinning room just off the kitchen, they enjoy a superior meal. She can tell Miguel enjoys showing off his culinary skills, and he deserves to. He's an excellent cook.

After dinner, Armida helps clean up the kitchen and they move to the living room area. The dramatic room is very much like a fine art gallery with glass fronted display cases containing a collection of woven baskets, pottery and an assortment of Native American craft items, rivaling some of those in the Taylor Museum's collection. In one corner there's a beautiful rounded kiva style, adobe fireplace. Navajo rugs are everywhere and white walls featured numerous paintings by New Mexico artists. Completing the visual feast is a mixture of colorful Kachina dolls and bronzes on pedestals. Armida sinks into one of the oversized leather armchairs.

"You have a great collection."

"This was my father's place and he collected a great deal of what's here," he told her. "I've only recently started to acquire a few pieces. Of course, my special interest is centered on early weavings; I plan on keeping a couple of the blankets you saw in Roswell."

"I bet, and one of them is the First Phase Ute."

"That's a given. It's a beautiful blanket."

"Have you given any thought to the Narbona Blanket?" Armida asks.

"No I'm waiting for your analysis."

"Well, I'm working on it but I haven't yet authenticated it."

Their conversation turns to an in-depth discussion of Native American crafts and the rightful ownership of old pieces. It's a stimulating exchange and Miguel is mesmerized by Armida's knowledge of southwestern history. For more than an hour they exchange views on a wide variety of subjects. Miguel finally asks. "Would you care for an after dinner drink? A little cognac perhaps? I've a five-year-old."

Miguel returns from the kitchen with two cognac glasses and sees Armida inspecting a beautiful little child's wearing blanket in a shadow box to the left of the fireplace.

"I think you'll like this," he says, as he hands the drink to her. "It's a superior pale. I love it and it's a brand not easy to find in New Mexico."

Armida inhales the cognac's aroma and takes a sip. "You're right. It's excellent. I've never tasted smoother."

Miguel watches as Armida sips at the cognac. He knows now that he wants this woman and is contemplating his next move when he again becomes aroused. Her nearness and the warm glow of the brandy are enough to make his decision. It's time to tell of his feelings. "I must tell you something, Miguel says. "I find you exciting. You're one of the most sensual, interesting women I've ever met."

Moving closer, he takes her empty glass and sets it by his own a nearby table, then takes her in his arms and looks deeply into her eyes. To his surprise she responds by offering her mouth again, just as before, but this time even though their lips touched lightly, Miguel finds himself responding to everything about her, his senses are alive. He's been attracted to many women and bedded his share. But Armida is different. He wants to be with her, look at her, listen to her and, of course, make love to her.

Armida lets him hold her close against him. Jose was the only man she ever knew. Her sex life with him was completely fulfilling. He was a very patient teacher and awakened her sexually. Under his tutorship she learned how to make love and enjoy it and she hasn't been with a man since he died. But she's not about to jump into bed with just anyone. Not that there hasn't been plenty of opportunities. But her upbringing and Catholic faith have always held her back. Now her sexuality, hidden away since his death, is taking over, and she finds she can't resist Miguel's embrace.

This time it's a deep, long, hungry kiss, which causes her to tremble with anticipation. When Miguel finally releases her, she clings to him, her head on his shoulder.

Armida lifts her head off his shoulder and looks at him with misty eyes. As Miguel kisses her once more and she touches his cheek lightly with her fingers. Miguel leans in slowly and again kisses her softly. Armida's eager body is now alive with desire as pent-up emotions grip her. The control, which has allowed her to remain celibate since Jose's death, melts away, and she is once again a sensual woman. She wants Miguel.

Opening her lips, she invites his tongue into her mouth with a teasing touch from hers. As he eagerly explores her mouth, she feels his fingertips move slowly up and down her arms. Then without warning, she guides his hands to her breasts and shudders as she feels their warmth through the sheer fabric of her blouse. As his hands cup her breasts, her nipples instantly became erect and she gives a little whimper.

"I want you. More than I imagined. Now." Without a word Miguel, leads her to his bedroom, and standing beside his bed, once more takes her in his arms.

For Armida there is no turning back now, and as the reality of where she is and what she was about to do strikes her, she tenses slightly for a moment. Sensing her hesitation Miguel backs up slightly. "There's a nice robe in the bathroom," he offers. "You might feel more comfortable in it."

Armida jumps at the chance. Safe inside the bathroom she attempts to get a grip on herself. She looks in the mirror and sees her flushed face. This is her chance to back out and she's grateful to Miguel for being astute enough to provide her an exit if she needs one. The bathroom is immaculately clean and very masculine. On the door hangs an expensive man's bathrobe, temptingly soft to her touch. For a brief moment, she considers backing out. Instead, she starts to undress.

In his bedroom Miguel waits, not knowing if she will return in his robe or decide not to undress. He removes his shoes and is considering what to do when the bathroom door opens, and Armida appears. As she moves toward him, it's obvious she wears only his robe. Once again she steps up close and he takes her in his arms.

For a brief time they simply hold each other.

Then Armida steps back, opens the front of his robe, again moving up against him. It's then, that Jose's training takes over and she starts to unbutton

Miguel's shirt. When she's finished, she kisses his neck as she pulls the shirt free from his pants and moves it off his shoulders, pressing her ample breasts against his bare chest in the process. He feels her warm hands and as she undoes his belt and slides his slacks and shorts over long, lean hips. Miguel's amazed. This woman, who seems so cool and aloof, is guiding him to his bed.

Armida lays him back on his pillow and explores his body. Now positioned above him, she kisses his shoulder, runs her fingers through his chest hair, lingering for a moment, and kisses his stomach as she moves downward. Then without warning she holds his erect manhood in her soft hands before positioning herself above him.

Armida gasps as she takes him inside her and repeatedly rises off of him then down again, each time driving him deeper. Finally she arches her back until he's in her fully and then bends forward to offer her breasts to his eager mouth, writhing with enjoyment. His thick pubic hair caresses her soft flesh as she moves against him. Leaning forward she gives a little whimpering sound as she buries her face in his chest and then seeks his lips once more.

Miguel marvelous as he watches her move above him, his tensions mounting in a cadence matching hers. Undulating against him, unable to bear the rushing excitement, she sucks in her breath and comes, with a hard jittery orgasm, which leaves her trembling as she falls limply against his chest.

Miguel realizes a sensual woman who knows how to please a man has made love to him. He's still in full bloom inside her, as she lies there exhausted. Knowing she was satisfied, he withdraws just as Armida rolls off him, reverses her position and finds his swollen member. Skillfully using her hands and mouth, as Jose taught her so many years ago, she easily brings him to a climax.

Afterwards, for what seems an eternity to Armida, they lay in each other's arms, not speaking. Then she feels Miguel's returning desire swelling against her leg. She turns toward him and reaching down takes hold. "My, my." she offers. "Look what we have here."

Miguel responds by moving to a position above her. In one fluid motion he's astride her. Then slowly lowers himself to kiss her neck, her breasts. When he feels her responding, his lips continue to explore her willing flesh. Finally, when she can take it no longer, Armida reaches up, and digging her fingernails into his back, pulls him close and invites him to enter her.

Hours later, the ring of his cell phone awakes Miguel. He answers groggily, "Miguel Jaramillo here."

Beside him in his bed, Armida half-asleep slowly wakes up becoming aware it's early morning. For a moment she doesn't realize where she is. Then as she becomes fully awake, she hears Miguel talking on the phone his voice low, deep and resonant. She lies there, enjoying the warm, wonderful feeling, one she has sorely missed, that of awaking next to a man. The images of the night before are still fresh in her mind, wonderful images of lovemaking with a virile man, exhilarates her. Last night brought back memories long ago curbed. She made love to him knowing full well how easily she could satisfy him, because she understands what a man needs. She recalls the intense feeling it gave her as she brought him to a climax and he spurted out his sticky ecstasy into her hands.

She lies there cozily, slowly becoming aware that Miguel is no longer talking on his cell phone but rather addressing her.

"Armida."

"Yes," replies Armida as she turns toward him.

"One of the two characters who left the weaving scrap in my van at Crownpoint, wants a meeting. He's offering to sell the rest of the weaving."

Armida's shocked. Now fully awake she can't believe the people responsible for the break-ins and Mary's injuries are acting as if nothing has happened. The gall of these characters is almost unreal. They should be in jail and here they are still trying to pedal the rest of the weaving.

With a quick kiss on her check, Miguel gets out of bed, dresses and tosses her his bathrobe. "If you'd like to shower, I'll see what I can rustle up for breakfast. Any preferences?"

"Black coffee and some toast would be fine."

"Will do. And by the way, good morning."

Miguel turns and disappears into the kitchen. Armida gets out of bed, picks up the robe and scurries into the bathroom.

Fifteen minutes later, fully freshened and dressed she enters the kitchen. Seeing that Miguel is busy at the stove, she moves up behind him and lightly kisses the back of his neck.

"Good morning. Thanks for last night."

"The pleasure was all mine." and grins. "Thank you."

Armida perches herself on the stool. "You should know you're the first man I've been with since my Jose died."

"I'm not sure what to say." Miguel says. "I'm flattered, but a little intimidated. I've never been with anyone quite like you.
 You realize I'm in love with you, don't you?"

"Miguel, I hope you'll be patient with me." Says Armida.

"I've got to free myself from the past before I can plan my future. Besides, we have some problems to deal with, not the least of which is our age difference. Lord knows I find you a fascinating man and want you. I can't remember a night as pleasurable as last night. If I had my way, we'd be in bed, again, right now. But please, be patient. Tell me about the call."

Miguel is delighted to hear how much she enjoyed last night, but her bringing up the potential problems of any relationship they might encounter disturbs him. Sure he has the same thoughts and knows full well there are obstacles to over come, but he doesn't want to think about it right now. Right now he simply wants to enjoy the moment. He decides not to comment on any difficulties they might face and discuss the phone call from Tomas. "The guy that called was a man named Tomas Reyes. He and his brother Jacinto are the ones who have the rest of the weaving," he tells her cracking two eggs in a pan.

"Are they the ones who hired the private detective who broke into my apartment and attacked Mary?"

"Yes, but of course this Tomas character claims they were not responsible for the attack on Mary. He says they hired the old detective to keep an eye on the sample piece they left with me. I think we should talk to the police detective before we do anything, don't you?"

"You're right," Armida agrees. "I have his card in my purse. I'll call him and find out what the situation is. If they really weren't involved in the break-in, I guess it's your call. I'll let you know what I find out."

Miguel's at ease as he moves about the kitchen. She watches him as he sets a plate with two slices of toast, a small dish of grape jelly, butter and a fresh cup of steaming coffee in front of her. Moments later he joins her with his bacon and eggs. They eat in silence and Armida begins to relax. She remembers all the times she and Jose enjoyed a quiet breakfast together. I need to get going." she tells Miguel when she finishes. "Let me help with the dishes."

"Go ahead. There isn't that much."

"OK. Next time I'll cook. I'd like to run for a few miles, and then I've got an appointment with Ricardo Flores. He's agreed to fill me in on Narbona and the killings at Canyon de Chelly. He's long-winded but very knowledgeable. I'll keep you posted on what I find out.

I have a feeling the old weaving could be of great historical significance and I really want to get started on proving it's the one in the photo. I could build a whole show around it."

"I should get to work, too," replies Miguel. "There's a large convention of physicians and surgeons in town this weekend and the gallery traffic should be up."

"Thanks again for last night, Mi Amante," she says, and stepping close, she takes his face in both hands while he stands there with his hands full of dishes. For a moment, she nibbles at his lips, then abruptly deepens the kiss. Then turning away, she picks up her purse. "I'll let myself out."

As Miguel finishes putting the rest of the dishes in the dishwasher, he realizes that he knows Armida is the one he wants to be with for the rest of his life. There's no question he's head over heels in love. At thirty-three he's like a schoolboy with his first crush. For many years he's wanted to find someone who will share his love of New Mexico and its fascinating history. But never in his wildest dreams did he ever think he would find someone like Armida. Lovely to look at, delightful to be with and great in bed.

CHAPTER 14

A five-mile run is exactly what Armida needs to get her mind back in focus and reset her priorities.

Now that Mary is recovering, she needs to concentrate on her work again. Of course, there is a new element; Miguel. For the last few years she has done pretty much as she wants but she realizes now that her life is about to change. She wants to include Miguel in that life but he poses a number of problems.

Armida's biological clock is running and her father constantly presses her to give him a grandson. With a towel around her neck, her run finished, Armida stretches, and leans back against her BMW's fender to cool off. Closing her eyes, her mind drifts back to her evening with Miguel, an evening so pleasurable she can hardly believe it happened. She and Miguel are so natural together she can't help but be excited contemplating what lies ahead for them.

She recalls how she actually hungered for Jose's body and now she feels the same kind of hunger for Miguel. Sex with Jose was an enjoyable, integral part of their marriage. For a long time, she believed that she would never find a man who could replace Jose. Now suddenly, when she least expected it, she has found someone who can do just that. Smiling to herself, she gets in her little red BMW and drives toward her Condo.

Right on time, Ricardo Flores walks into Armida's office at the University. He's short and squatty with a beard that is salt and pepper colored, like his hair. He looks as if he's slept in his suit and could still use a little sleep. His thick horn-rimmed glasses make his dark eyes look out of proportion to his face and he needs a haircut.

"*Buenõs Dias, Dõna* Valenzuela."

"*Hõla, Senõr* Flores." Armida replies, getting up from her desk. "Thank you for coming, have a seat."

Ricardo slips into a chair opposite her desk. "I heard about the break-in and attack on your lab assistant. How is she doing?"

"Mary's doing well, the doctor says she'll recover and there should be no permanent damage. They caught the guy who did it, and there was nothing missing from my apartment. I guess it's a sign of the times. What have you been up to?"

"Same old routine. But I understand you've got another book coming out," he says, crossing his legs and settling back in his seat. "I'm so proud of you, Armida. Like you, I believe the world needs to learn more about this state because it's so fascinating." Then proceeds to tell her about a three state speaking tour he made recently and the research he's presently engaged in to gather materials for a book, an in-depth study of Santa Fe.

"It's amazing how few people realize that Santa Fe was a thriving city for many years before the Pilgrims landed at Plymouth Rock," he offers. "I've always found it curious American historians have steadfastly chosen to deny the historical significance of the Spanish in the discovery and settlement of the New World."

As usual, when Ricardo reverts to this subject he becomes vehement. "They've repeatedly emphasized the pilgrims' era and only occasionally mentioned the role played by the Spanish. That's one of the reasons I find myself regularly compelled to speak out."

Armida's accustomed to Ricardo going on and on. Furthermore she agrees with him. She knows they must continue to write and speak out until American historians finally acknowledge the fact that the Spanish have made important contributions to America's cultural development.

"Oh I think it's coming about." Armida offers. And she does. "It all started in the seventies when Mexican American's began to look into their heritage. Newly defined as "Latinos," they started to affirm the existence of a Spanish history in their writings. Today these immigrants are largely isolated from South America and Mexico and need an American heritage with which to cling. They want acceptance by American society and are attempting to dispel the image of an oppressed group. It's my personal feeling great progress has been made both politically and economically for the Mexican," continues Armida. "You and I are representatives of such progress."

"You speak as well as you write," Ricardo tells her. "What can I do for you?"

"I need to know what you can tell me about Narbona." she says. Reaching into a drawer she retrieves the file folder on the Narbona blanket and lays it, unopened, it front of her on her desk.

"Well, how much history do you want?" he asks. "I taught a class on Narbona last semester."

"I've got the time, professor. Go for it. Then I have something to show you."

"Well, as I told my class, Mexico won its independence from Spain in 1821, and gained jurisdiction over New Mexico. Under Mexican rule sporadic violence escalated into nearly constant warfare. Mexicans disregarded numerous treaties and constantly conducted raids into Navajo Indian country and took slaves. They forced Navajo women to weave blankets. I believe you have one in your museum collection. Although woven on Navajo looms these blankets combined the characteristics of both Navajo and Mexican weaving."

"You're right," Armida replies. "I featured one of those blankets on the cover of my last book, which covered Rio Grande textiles."

"Yes I know," responds Ricardo. Getting up from his chair, he begins to pace back and forth like he does in his lectures.

"It was during this time the Navajos, on horseback, retaliated and raided towns and settlements to recover slaves. In the process they also plundered and took livestock."

He goes on to explain that, by 1864, the warfare and an advancing

American army finally convinced the Mexicans to give up the territory of New Mexico without a fight. Arriving in Santa Fe the American commander, Brigadier General Stephen Kearny, announced the Mexicans who stayed would be considered American citizens and promised to protect both them and the Catholic Church from the Indians. However, he failed to promise to protect the Indians against slave raids.

"My great grandfather wrote about this in his journal," Armida interjects. "Perhaps you would like to read it sometime."

"I'd love to see it." Responds Ricardo, who has stopped pacing and again taken his seat. "Less than three months after their arrival in New Mexico the American soldiers began a campaign against the Navajo Nation. Narbona, one of the powerful elder Navajos, learned the Mexicans were settling around Mount Taylor. Navajo leaders wanted to attack the settlements and drive them away from Mount Taylor. He knew how powerful the army was and negotiated the treaty at Bear Springs. The treaty was supposed to protect the Navajos from settlement and slave raids and promised to open up trade with them."

"Just one of many treaties that were not honored by Washington," comments Armida.

"Precisely, all the Navajos elders, like Narbona, and the Americans who signed the treaty were sincere, but you're correct, this treaty and others, which followed, were doomed."

"We both know it's true. Broken treaties soon became the rule, not the exception, and after the New Mexico territory was officially annexed to the United States in 1848 the Navajos were in complete disarray. The situation continued to deteriorate until the American army, leaving only two companies, was recalled to fight in the Civil War. Narbona and his people were then faced with the American governor, Colonel James Macrae Washington, who requested the New Mexican people form their own civilian war parties to conduct raids against the Navajos."

"In 1849, at the Canyon de Chelly, Colonel Washington was said to have shot Narbona in a dispute over a stolen horse. The death of Narbona triggered a bloody war between the Navajos and Territorial forces. This war culminated in the eventual defeat of the Navajo nation and their being taken from the lands and imprisoned at the infamous "Bosque Redondo" in Eastern New Mexico, a barren water less area that became a death camp. It was one of the saddest times in New Mexico history," Ricardo says thoughtfully. "No wonder Narbona became a hero to the Navajo people."

Armida jumps at the chance to speak. "I knew I had heard his name mentioned, but until now I wasn't fully aware of his stature among the Navajos."

With that comment, she hands Ricardo the letter and photograph. While Ricardo studies the picture and letter, she gets up, puts on a pair of white cotton gloves and takes the old blanket from a file cabinet, removes it from a cotton cover and spreads it out on her desk.

"My God." Blurts out Ricardo, looking up from the photo. "This is Narbona. I've seen other photos of him."

Ricardo continues to study the letter of provenance and then, without touching it, studies the old blanket spread out on the desk in front of him. Pointing to the hole in the blanket he says. "This sure looks like the bullet hole in the photo. Have you done any testing on it"

"Not yet. What with the break-in and trips to the hospital, I haven't had time and then I want to do a DNA test to see if that's blood around the hole. I'd like to find a relative of Narbona and see if I can come up with a match."

"Well, his great grandson lives in Red Rock, Arizona," Ricardo offers. "He's very old but I think he's still around. I can get in touch through a teacher I know there. Let me arrange it. This is a fabulous discovery. Where in the world did you come by this?"

"It's on loan from a friend. I'm hoping he'll donate the weaving to our museum," replies Armida.

"What a find. This is a priceless piece of New Mexico's history. How many people know about it?" Once again Ricardo is up and pacing in front of her desk. His rumpled appearance now even more disheveled as he makes a futile attempt to keep his unkept hair out of his line of site.

"I've decided to keep our findings confidential until I verify the age and get a DNA match." Armida explains.

"I plan to start my testing Monday. If you can get me a DNA sample from Narbona's great grandson, I would really appreciate it,"

"I'll get in touch with the teacher and let you know right away."

Armida carefully re-folds the blanket, places it back in it's protective covering and returns it to the file cabinet behind her. She turns back to Ricardo. "I really appreciate your keeping this under your hat for the present, Ricardo. I hope my research verifies its authenticity and the DNA establishes a link to Narbona."

"You have my fullest confidence." Getting up and trying to act causal, Ricardo asks, "How about lunch some time?"

"I'd really like that. However, you should know I'm seeing someone." Armida understands that he's probably under the impression that she's not dating. Everyone who knows her realizes she has never fully gotten over Jose's death.

"I'm pleased to hear that," he says. "Anyone I know?"

"He's not an academician." Armida tells him, not certain just how much she should say about her relationship to Miguel at this stage, but determined not to keep him a secret. "He's a Latino art dealer. But, I'd still enjoy having lunch with you. Let's keep in touch."

As Ricardo leaves her office, Armida can't help but realize this is the first time she has publicly acknowledged Miguel. Knowing Ricardo, she's certain that word of her new relationship will be all over the campus by nightfall. Not an unpleasant thought, but then there will be the inevitable questions.

Armida is using a Jewelers loop to study another old child's blanket when her phone rings.

"Good afternoon, Professor Valenzuela. This is J.T. Romero. Do you have a minute?"

"Certainly, Señŏr Romero. What can I do for you?"

"We've got a confession from an old detective, Armando Peralta," J.T. tells her. "He's the man who was hired by Tomas and Jacinto Reyes to break into your apartment.
And confirms the old detective was the one who left the weaving sample with Miguel Jaramillo and attacked Mary Chavez. "

I'm not positive we can charge the Reyes brothers with anything, but we're getting a search warrant and my hope is we will find them in possession of Indian artifacts." he continues. "The brothers claim they never told Armando to break-in or assault Mary. It's their word against his. But we can charge Armando. I'll need you to come down and sign some paper work. Armando's going to plead guilty, so I don't know what the District Attorney will do with him."

"You mean he's going to be able to plea bargain his way out of this?" Armida doesn't bother to hide the fact that she is outraged.

"They'll probably plead him out," continues J.T. "That's the way the system works nowadays. The sooner you come down, the better."

"Has anyone told my father yet?"

"Not that I know of."

"Well, I intend to," Armida fumes. "And he's not going to like it. I can tell you that. Mary is almost like family and he's not going to be pleased if they let this man plead his way out of jail time."

"I could be wrong," J.T. tells her. "But I see so much of this kind of thing these days. I'll bet they do let him plead."

"I'll be down there in an hour," is her sharp reply. "In the mean time, I'm going to call my father and see what he thinks about this."

By the time Armida arrives at police headquarters, word has came down from Carlos Valenzuela to the Senate Majority leader, to the Mayor of Albuquerque, to the District Attorney, and then to the Police Chief who informs J.T. Romero there will be no plea bargaining in this case. Carlos Valenzuelas' political influence is about to take center stage in court.

CHAPTER 15

Back in her apartment after what had been a long day, Armida was exhausted. When she arrived at police headquarters, she was assured the District Attorney had decided there would be no plea bargaining in her case, which came as no surprise, considering her father had came unwound when she told him about the probability of a plea. She's preparing a snack before retiring when the phone rings and since her caller ID indicates its Miguel; she's quick to answer it.

"Buenõs noches, Mi Amante."

"Buenõs noches, Mi Amor. How was your day?"

"Not that great. I spent most of the afternoon down at police headquarters with detective Peralta."

"You sound tired. I have to go down there tomorrow morning. I need to give them a formal statement. Peralta tells me they plan on prosecuting Armando, the old private investigator who caused so much trouble."

"Serves him right. Mary could have been hurt much worse. Thank God, she wasn't."

"So do you know when she will be released from the hospital?"

"Her doctor says in a couple of more days. Then she's going to stay with my father until she can go back to work. Jesse, her son, has been staying there since the attack and our housekeeper, Juanita Garcia, is there to help."

"Great. Listen, I don't want to keep you up, but Tomas Reyes called again and wants to meet. I asked Detective Peralta about the Reyes brothers and he said they are facing numerous charges, and if we are going to find out anything further about the scrap, we better hurry before they get picked up. They may not know they have a serious problem so, I'll call them tonight. The scrap of weaving is evidence in the case against Armando and won't be returned until after the trial.
I imagine the Reyes brothers are aware of that."

"Why don't you see if they can take some good photos of the rest of the weaving and we'll take a look at them?" Armida suggested. With what I've already found out, the photos might answer a lot of our questions."

"Sounds like a good idea to me," Miguel replies. "Let me know when you find out what they want to do."

As she hangs up the phone, after agreeing to have lunch with Miguel, Armida decides it's time for a long hot bath.

The next morning, after an hour session with Detective Peralta, Miguel learns there really is a good chance the Reyes brothers could be in serous trouble. J.T. confirmed they are also under suspicion for trading in illegal Indian antiquities, whereupon Miguel returned to the Albuquerque gallery and hurriedly calls Tomas Reyes.

"I spoke with Detective Peralta," he tells him, "and he told me the District Attorney is holding the scrap of weaving you left me as evidence. They may keep it for months."

"I just heard." Tomas says gruffly. "I really wish you hadn't given my property to the lady at the university. The piece wasn't yours to give. You caused a lot of problems."

All things considered, Miguel can't believe the bastard is chewing on him. But he decides to keep his cool and make his move, particularly since he needs more information on the rug.

"Since you can't offer the complete weaving, I'm not sure I'm really interested," he tells Tomas. "However, if you want to take some decent photos of the weaving and drop them by my gallery with any provenance you have, I'll take a look. You don't need to bring the whole weaving. I obtained the information I needed from the scrap. But I would like to see the whole design and find out the dimensions."

Miguel waits; hoping Tomas will take the bait. He's pleasantly surprised when he agrees.

"I have excellent photos. There is no provenance. It's a found weaving. What time does the gallery close?"

"We're on summer hours. The gallery is open until 7:00 P.M. If I'm not there, leave them with Chris."

Tomas agrees. "Just don't take too long to get back to me. You're not the only one interested in the weaving."

"Look." Miguel says in an impatient, warning voice. "I'll get back to you soon enough. You can depend on that."

The following morning, Miguel is seated at a sidewalk table outside Dee's with the photos spread out in front of him as he waits for Armida.

Looking up later he spots Armida hurrying toward him. She's wearing a turquoise broom skirt with matching suede boots, a squash blossom necklace and matching earrings that feature hummingbirds. He instantly recognizes the set as the work of the famous Zuni Singer family. Armida's braless breasts seem to be in motion beneath the soft, white fabric of her of-the-shoulder peasant blouse. As she draws near, he thinks, *Damn! She is one beautiful lady.* Shuffling the pictures back into a stack, he gets up to greet her. "*Buenõs Dias.*"

"*Buenõs Dias.*" Armida kisses his cheek lightly and sits down. "I'm sorry I'm late. Busy day at the lab. We got in a new batch of textiles for consideration."

"No problem, I've only been here a few minutes myself. That's a lovely set of Singer work you're wearing."

"Thanks, they were presents from my late husband."

Miguel once again finds reason to realize how lucky he is to have Armida's company. He had noticed several men staring at her as she approached. He knows well how they must envy him as she sits down at his table.

"Our gallery has handled the Singer Family's work since the mid-70's," he offers.

Their waiter serves them blue corn chips and salsa and takes their orders. While they wait, Miguel passes Armida the stack of photos.

"Here, take a look at these, I've never seen anything like this pattern."

Armida carefully studies the photos, one by one and then making no comment, she goes through the stack again. Finally, she sits back. "I'm sure the weaving was done by a Navajo weaver. You're right, the pattern is very unusual. It appears to be a combination of designs and jumbled, odd shapes. The style is Rio Grande and I've seen similar backgrounds on several occasions. As a matter of fact, we have an example in our collection."

Armida continues, "Navajo women were often taken as slaves, and they were forced to weave for their masters. The result was this style of weaving. Woven on a vertical Navajo loom as they were, the designs were almost always heavily influenced by their Spanish captors. But in all my travels I've never seen such a hodgepodge of shapes and symbols in a single Navajo weaving. I'm at a loss.
I don't have the vaguest idea what the design represents." Armida immediately senses Miguel's disappointment.

"How sure are you of the age?" he asks.

"I believe it was woven around 1850, about the time the Mexican army abandoned New Mexico and headed home." Armida is now standing. She has taken her glasses from her purse and spread all the pictures out on the table. She is intently looking at them again when the waiter arrives with their meal. Gathering them back in a stack she sits back down. "It's even possible it's earlier, possibly 1800 to 1825. The thing is, a couple of the designs appear to be Tabira Black-on-white like the ones I've seen on old Rio Grande pottery shards. Very strange."

Armida hands him back the photos. "I'd like to show these to Ricardo Flores. It's so non-typical. Maybe he can give us an idea what the design represents. He's out of town but he should be back early next week."

"Sounds like an excellent idea, I heard him speak last year. He's a little long-winded but very knowledgeable. Here, take them to him."

Armida slips the photos into her purse and they start lunch. When their sopaipillas and honey are served for desert, Armida says, "I need to use the ladies' room. I'll be right back."

Miguel gets up quickly and Armida, purse in hand, leaves for the restrooms.

Her toilette finished, she takes her cell phone out and calls her father. "Hola, Papa."

"Hola, muchacha."

"Papa, I'm coming up tonight and I need to know if I could invite someone to come for dinner Sunday? I'd like a chance to show off my cooking."

"Certainly. Mi Casa es su casa. Anyone I know?" Armida detects a little surprise in her father's voice.

"Yes. Miguel Jaramillo."

There's a moment of silence. "Of course, I'll tell Juanita. If you want anything special, you should call her."

"Will do. I'm at lunch. I've got to go. Te amo, Papa."

"Y yo Te amo, Mi Hijita."

"I'm going up to the rancho after work today," she tells Miguel when she returns to the table. "I need to check on the grapes and spend a little time with my father. Would you like to come for supper Sunday evening?"

An invitation for supper at the Valenzuela rancho, thinks Miguel. *What would Carlos think of that?* Carlos' reputation and his own research indicates this may provoke an awkward situation, but Armida has asked and there's no way he's going to turn down her invitation. "Certainly." he says. "I'm headed up to check on the gallery later today, and I'll spend the night in Santa Fe. I have a little apartment near the plaza. I'd like to come up to the rancho. What time?"

"We'll have supper about six, but if you come a little earlier we can spend some time in the vineyard."

"Sounds like fun. I know very little about wine making but I do enjoy a good vintage."

"If I had my way, I'd be a full time vintner. Perhaps you'll learn something."

"I'm sure I will."

Once outside, Miguel takes her in his arms and instantly his mouth is on hers. She responds to the gentle, persuasive kiss. When he draws back, his hands are on her face, his fingers lightly brushes her cheekbones then trail down her neck.

"I'll see you Sunday afternoon, thanks for the invitation."

Armida can still feel the warmth of his kiss as he moves away toward his gallery. It's a nice feeling.

Back at his desk, Miguel wonders what Carlos Valenzuela will say. Surely Armida obtained his permission before asking him to come up. In any event, her invitation is a major step for Armida, one sure to have consequences. In fact, he gains a lot of confidence as he thinks about it. *Maybe he does have a chance with the beautiful lady. Sunday will be an interesting day, a very interesting day!*

CHAPTER 16

Armida is in the kitchen with Juanita preparing posole when Carlos comes in. Earlier, over breakfast, he was silent, clearly lost in thought. He'd been with a breeder since 9:00 a.m., here for the servicing of his mare by Carlos's Golden Boy.

How did it go?" Armida asks.

"Everything went fine," her father says, looking a little peaked as he stands there. "Golden Boy was ready as usual. He's the best I've ever owned, a true champion. Got any coffee?"

"Of course. Wana taste the posole?" Armida decided to fix posole for supper because she considers this slow cooked, traditional dish of hominy, pork and chicken one of her best.

Carlos takes a seat at the table, and Juanita sets a cup of coffee in front of him. Armida dips a spoon into the posole, blows on it, and hands it to her father.

"Very good," Carlos tells her, licking the spoon. But it could use a little more cumin."

"You got it."

"What makes you think a Latino will appreciate posole?"

"Come on, Papa, that's uncalled for. By the way, Miguel is one Latino you better damn well get used to."

Armida is upset, and the fire in her eyes gets Carlos' attention as she whirls away and returns to her cooking. Carlos realizes his attempt at a joke has fallen on deaf ears and says. "Hey. Wait a minute, can't you take a little joke? I like Miguel. I didn't realize how much you care for him. When did all this happen?"

"I should've warned you," Armida answers. Disturbed, but not totally surprised by his gruff attitude. She's been worried about how to break the news of her deep feelings for Miguel, realizing there is probably no good time to tell her father.

She looks Carlos straight in the eye, and decides this is as good a time as any. "Papa, I'm in love with Miguel. Seriously in love."

Carlos is silent. Of all the things he desires, at the top of his list, is to see Armida happily married. He desperately wants a male heir as well but, until now, he never even considered the possibility that Armida could fall in love with a Latino.

"I'll have to think about this," he says sullenly. "I'll need some time. You know I only want what's best for you." Without further comment, Carlos gets up and leaves the kitchen.

Armida knows Carlos's prejudice toward those not of Castillian blood is one of the hurdles she will have to get over, but now she's told him how she feels. The posole done, she leaves the rest of the meal to Juanita, and with mixed emotions, goes to her bedroom to change.

***

When Miguel drives out to the Valenzuela rancho that afternoon, there's a package containing a beautiful silver concha belt featuring hummingbirds by Elie Singer on the seat next to him. The Singer family's delicate inlays are considered the finest examples of modern Zuni Indian work, and this belt is an excellent piece. Miguel hums to himself as he imagines the little humming birds bouncing along on Armida's swaying hips. He called ahead and as he drives up to the Valenzuela casa, Armida is waiting on the front porch. Today she wears a blue denim jumper and jacket embroidered with petroglyph figures. She's a startling sight, even in what Armida probably considers work clothes, she looks very appealing. Miguel gets out of his van, and rather than clasping her outstretched hand, gives her the package.

"What's this?" she asks him, as she gives him a quizzical look, then a warm smile.

"Something I thought you might enjoy."

"You shouldn't have."

"Open it."

When Armida removes the concha from the tissue she grasped, "Oh, my God. How beautiful. It's Singer, isn't it?"

"Yes, this is Elie's work. I think the squash and earrings you have are her brother Tommy's work. I'm glad you're pleased. I think her work is even more delicate than Tommy's.

Armida hooks the belt around her waist, takes his face in both hands, and gives him a long, deep kiss. "It's been a long time since a man gave me a gift," she says softly. "And this is certainly one of the most beautiful I've ever received. Thank you."

Armida thinks her ancestors must be spinning in their graves at the very notion that she has accepted an expensive gift from a man she's not engaged to, a man who isn't even Castilian.

"It's not nearly as beautiful as the lady wearing it."

Armida grabs him by the hand; "I'll thank you properly later. Let's have a look at the vineyard."

This time, Armida has a golf cart parked around a corner behind the casa. As she gets behind the steering wheel, she beckons to Miguel, "Jump aboard."

Armida drives on a graveled path past the corrals and to the right of a row of vines. After a quarter of a mile, they stop in front of a long wooden shed. On the way, Miguel has noticed dozens of laborers tending the vines.

"You've got quite a crew working," he says.

"Yes, and we have an excellent foreman who supervises them. This is nothing. You should see them work when we prune the vines."

"I'm not familiar with the process. What's so special about the pruning?"

"We prune the vines to train them. Properly pruned, they also become more resistant to disease. Our efforts are rewarded with better distribution of the bearing wood to increase grape production."

Armida stops the cart. "Let's walk, I'll show you."

As they stroll down a row of vines, Armida points out how the vines have been cared for and the results they hope for in a vintage. Occasionally, picking a grape, she holds it up to the sun to peer through its translucent globe before tasting it. Her enthusiasm enchants Miguel. He realizes how serious she is about viniculture and can't help but wonder if Carlos will ever give her the chance to take over the vineyard.

After a half-hour, they return to a shed, and Armida unlocks the door. The shed is built against a bluff and to Miguel' surprise the entrance leads into a very large cave filled with winemaking equipment. As they walk by the machinery, Armida explains each machine's use in the wine making process.

"Our harvest begins right away. The grapes will be brought here, dumped into the grape hopper, and conveyed to the destemmer."

She goes on to explain that inside the destemmer, the paddles strike the clusters of grapes to separate them from their stems. How the loose grapes fall through holes in the sleeve of the machine, and down into a crusher which lightly breaks the skin so the pressing will be easier.

"The white grapes are pumped into the winery to be pressed," she continues. "The red ones are placed in a fermentation tank for several days, then pressed. Our press uses a bladder that gently presses the grapes against the bottom of the press. The juice runs out through grids inside the tank into the gray pipe you see there, then is pumped to stainless steel storage tanks. The grape seeds and skins are emptied into a hopper under the press and are conveyed outside where they are used as livestock feed or mulch."

"I thought wine was stored in wooden casks," Miguel says.

"It is. After pressing, we transfer the wine into oak casks to age for fourteen to twenty-four months. Our wine is racked many times during the aging process. During this process we look, listen, smell and taste the wine to check its progress. Young red wine is generally very tannic and not very pleasant to drink. Aging helps to smooth out the tannins."

Miguel is fascinated as she explains the difference in processing white grapes. Armida is in a wine making zone, obviously talking about something she loves. When they reach the end of the processing room, she opens a large pair of wooden doors, turns on the lights, and Miguel sees dozens of barrels in racks two high. The underground temperature is cool, and the place smells wonderful. Toward the end of the aisle are a few rows of inclined racks of upside down bottles.

"We make a small offering of sparkling wine each year from the white grapes," Armida explains. "These bottles contain some of our best young blended wines to which we've added a little yeast and sugar. Here they are going through their second fermentation. Adding yeast and sugar to the young wine causes the conversion of sugar into alcohol. The bubbles which are generated can't escape into the air because the bottles are capped."

Picking up one of the bottles, Armida holds it upward toward an overhead light. "See the sedimentation in the neck?"

"Yes, how do you get rid of it?"

"During the aging every one of these bottles is lifted and twisted like this every day." She demonstrates, and the twisting accelerates the particle separation as it spins in her hands. "When we decide the wine has peaked, the neck is frozen in brine so the sediment can be removed. The cap is taken off and the frozen sediment slides out, with little or no loss of wine. Then we top off the residual with a little brandy and recap it before storing it upside down." Armida points to another set of racks. "Then we store them over there."

"I had no idea how much labor is required," Miguel says.

"There are, of course, more modern ways to produce a champagne type wine, but if we place a Valenzuela label on a vintage, we want it to represent the best we are capable of and you can't beat the traditional way of creating a fine wine."

"Well, it's certainly well known how fine the Valenzuela wines are," Miguel replies.

"As early as 1602 New Mexico vineyards produced wine from mission grapes," she explains. We were the first wine-producing region in America, a full century before wine-grape planting in California. As a matter of fact, the 1880 New Mexico census showed 3,150 acres of vineyards under cultivation in New Mexico. Ours were some of those acres. A disastrous flood in 1897, followed by severe drought and Prohibition, almost wiped out the vineyards in our state. But since 1970, a number of foreign winemakers have invested in New Mexico plants."

"I didn't realize we have foreign winemakers?"

"Certainly." As they walked back toward the entrance she continues. "We now have French, Italian, German and Swiss winemakers here. New Mexico wines are fast becoming popular in the American wine market also. Here at our rancho, we experience a phenomenon in grape growing most desert regions do not. The sun is very intense because of cloudless skies. Also, the high altitude causes nighttime temperatures to drop 35-40 degree F. below daytime temperatures. Arid grape growing regions do not experience such contrasts in temperatures."

Miguel willingly listens and learns. "Now I understand why you want to give it a try. Sounds like the timing is right. I've grown to like a number of local wines but I had no idea they were becoming so popular. I rarely see any Valenzuela label in the stores."

"Almost all of our production is purchased by connoisseurs and restaurants because we are a very small winery," Armida answers. "I'd like to increase our acreage and become a player in that market. But enough of this, let's get back to the casa. I didn't mean to bore you with all this information."

Armida leads the way out of the shed door. Following close behind, Miguel says, "You could never bore me. I find you a fascinating woman, and I've learned more about wine making today than I ever thought I would know."

"I'm so glad you came," Armida murmurs as they reach the golf cart.

Miguel takes her in his arms and they kiss, a nice, warm kiss. "I can't stop thinking about you." He says, holding her close. I must tell you that I'm in love with you. Armida please, let me know what you feel. I need to know."

"*Si, Mi Corazon.*" She tosses her dark hair back from her face, her eyes sparkling with delight. "I've told my father that I love you, let's go have supper and face him together."

In his study Carlos Valenzuela is finishing up the paper work on Golden Boy's stud service. This is the second time the Alvarez family has used his Golden Boy. Just two years ago, the same mare produced a spectacular foal, one of the many Golden Boy has sired. Like his ancestors, Carlos takes great pride in his horses. His people have owned this land, at the headwaters of the Rio Grande and Pecos rivers, since 1790. When the United States occupied the territory of New Mexico in 1846 the Valenzuela land holdings were virtually isolated. With high mountains on the north and west and long stretches of semi-desert country to the east and south, the Valenzuela properties had remained geographically remote until the early 1900's when modern roads allowed easy access. Before that, the journey to Santa Fe, the nearest city at a distance of approximately 50 miles by the most direct route, had taken several difficult days.

Carlos's grandfather, Hernando, acquired his wealth from raising sheep and horses as well as producing wine to gain the influence that both Carlos's father, and Carlos enjoyed. Carlos liked being a Valenzuela. It was an old name, a good name, a strong name and now, with no son of his own, he was faced with a daughter who was considering changing it to a Latino one. Carlos was struggling with the prospect. He loves his daughter, and without question, her happiness is the most important thing in his life. But he's always thought she would at least marry a Castilian and keep his family's Spanish heritage intact. He knows Miguel is a good businessman and is well respected. But he isn't Castilian.

Although Carlos has developed a satisfactory pattern of accommodation for dealing with Latinos, he and his close relatives rarely intermarry with Latinos. Among the Castilian people of the area Carlos is considered a *patron*, by all counts, a rare individual in today's New Mexican society. He has been shrewd enough to keep the family resources intact and over the years converted a number of them into more lucrative channels, no longer running sheep or cattle except for a few kept by his workers for milk and wool. He's made solid investments in commercial real estate and still holds title to all the land in the original land grant.
By any standard he's a successful, wealthy man and Armida is his sole heir, something he must consider, now that she is in love again. He's deep in thought when Armida and Miguel enter his study.

Dragging his attention back to the moment, Carlos stands and takes Miguel's hand with seeming reluctance.

"*Como Te gusto el turno del de vina?*" Carlos asks.

Armida admonishes him. "Speak English Papa."

"Armida has just taken me on a fascinating tour of the winery," Miguel says quickly, anxious to defuse an awkward moment. "I didn't realize how labor intensive it is."

"Few people do," Carlos tells him, not meeting his eyes. You should be here when the picking starts."

"The Merlot look great and the new French-American White Hybrids are doing well, Armida says, keeping her voice low but under control. "This looks like a good year."

"Will you be able to get some time off for the picking?" Carlos asks her gruffly.

"Papa, you know I wouldn't miss our harvest. I've already arranged the time. Juanita has the table set up in the patio. Shall we go?"

Supper is quiet. It's obvious, there is more than a little tension between Armida and her father. After appetizers of chicken-chili pate and cornmeal puffs the posole is served. "Your posole is great," Miguel exclaims. "What's your secret?"

"I don't have any idea," Carlos answers stiffly. "We've always fixed it like this."

"You must use more than one meat," Miguel says with a puzzled look. "It tastes a little like chicken."

"Your palate is well trained," Armida tells him. "We used both chicken and pork loin. Some people make it with pork only. Perhaps that's the difference."

"Maybe I can talk you out of the recipe?"

"Perhaps. I'm not sure I've ever seen it written down. I'll see what I can do."

Armida turns to her father, "Papa, Miguel is a great cook. He studied at the Culinary Institute in Albuquerque. He fixes a mean fajita."

Carlos makes no comment. As soon as he finishes his meal, he excuses himself, saying he has some bookwork to catch up. Both Miguel and Armida are aware of a sense of relief as soon as he leaves the table.

"Do you ride?" Armida asks as they get up from the table. "Because I have something I would like to share with you." Just give me a minute to change. Rosa will bring you a brandy."

She returns, ten minutes later, dressed in riding britches and boots. Miguel is sitting on the terrace, nursing his drink. She leans close, gives him a light kiss on the cheek. "Ready?" she asks. "Come on, let's go."

When they arrive at the corrals, Armida points to one of the two beautiful saddled horses. "You'll like Pancho. He's one of my favorites." Armida mounts with the ease of an experienced horsewoman and Miguel, although not as nimble, manages to get into the saddle without embarrassing himself.

Their ride takes them past the vineyard and up the side of a hill. The late afternoon is typical for this part of northern New Mexico with a light breeze out of the West, cooling the temperature slightly. Miguel is enjoying the ride when they come upon a little meadow surrounded by quaking aspens, whose leaves have just started to turn to red.

"This is it," she says, leading her horse to a nearby hitch rack, dismounts and takes a saddlebag from behind her saddle.

Miguel is right behind her as she moves up a little trail toward a large rock ledge, where hidden below an overhanging ledge is a hot spring, steam rising from its surface. Next to the spring, under a pinon tree, are a split log bench, worn smooth from use, and a small table.

Opening the saddlebag, Armida takes out two plastic cups, a bottle of wine and two towels. "Help me off with my boots,"

As she holds onto a branch overhead for balance, Miguel grasps the heel of the fine leather boot and pulls it off, repeated the process with the other, then watches as Armida slowly removes the rest of her clothing and slips into the hot spring.

"Pour me a cup of wine and come on in," she tells him, her eyes twinkling, "the water's wonderful." Armida always knows what she wants, and it was clear that she wants him now.

"This is my little hideaway," Armida says as he settles down beside her. I've come here since I was a little girl."

The water temperature is hot but not too hot and Miguel begins to feel aroused.

"The water temperature is always the same," Armida offers, "In the winter with snow on the ground, its perfection. And then, as she moves closer, she murmurs, "Would you like to make love to me?"

Afterwards Armida takes his hand playfully, and tugs him out of the spring. Back at the bench Armida dries off, making a production of drying her hair while standing in front of him naked, her body aglow in the late afternoon sunlight. "I always find the cool air stimulating after the hot water, don't you?" she asks.

Miguel hears the desire in her voice. All his life he had heard tales of hot-blooded Castilian women and now he is with one and enjoying every moment.

They ride back to the Valenzuela casa under a dramatic New Mexico sunset. As the sun lowers, the western sky turns a brilliant red and appears to be on fire.

Heading back to Santa Fe, Miguel can't remember a day as exciting as this one or a woman like Armida. Like him she shares his love of New Mexico and its history, not only is she brilliant, but she's so full of life that she makes him feel more like a man than any woman he's ever known. No wonder he's fallen so deeply in love, so quickly. He knows he must have her for his wife, no matter how much her father might disapprove.

CHAPTER 17

All during Sunday, Armida tries to get her father to talk to her about Miguel, to no avail. She understands her father's pride in their Castilian heritage and his reluctance to condone her feelings toward Miguel. But she also knows in spite of his lack of support, she will continue seeing Miguel. She needs him. She wants to belong to him completely. There's something almost frightening about her unquenchable thirst for his body. And she knows, no matter what her father thinks, all Miguel needs to do is to ask and she will be his.

Monday morning Armida clears her calendar, and asks Ricardo Flores to meet her for lunch in the University's cafeteria. When she enters, she spots him waiting near the door. Chatting about grapes and vineyards, they move through the serving line and find seats near the window overlooking the campus quadrangle. The campus is alive with students, many of whom are gathered in small groups using this lull in studies to plan the weekend's homecoming activities. While they eat, Armida brings Ricardo up to date on her research concerning the weaving. When they're finished, she hands him several photos of the rest of the scrap.

"Have you ever seen anything like this?" she asks.

Ricardo carefully studies the photos for a long time. "I can't say I have," he says finally. "Certain elements of the design are very unusual. In fact, this is the strangest combination I've ever seen. However, there's something vaguely familiar about the abstract center design. This symbol is similar to Kohka images I've seen on early pottery fragments, but somehow this one seems incomplete."

Armida points to another area in one of the pictures, "Isn't this symbol the one Navajos used to represent the 'Long Gowns,' their name for Franciscan monks?"

"You know, I believe so. What you need to do is to show these photos to a Navajo Singer. I know of one who might be able to help. He lives off Old Hwy. 666 north of Tohatchi near the Toadlena trading post up in the Chukka Mountains. He served as a code talker in World War II and goes by the name of Uaroba."

Armida knows Miguel will be familiar with the code talkers who were among the most revered elders of the Navajo Nations. Long unrecognized because of the continued value of their language as a security-classified code, they have finally been acknowledged by the United States government. Their skill and courage saved both American lives and military engagements in World War II.

"The operator of the trading post there can put you in touch with him,"

Ricardo concludes. "I believe the trading post is operated by a man named Jacinto Suspan. I interviewed Uaroba a couple years ago. If he's still alive, he might be able to give you a clue what these symbols mean. They could be some kind of Navajo cryptology. If so, this old Holy Man might know. It could be worth a try. I wish I was more help."

"No, no," Armida pleads. "You've been a great help. I hadn't thought of a Navajo Medicine Man. I've spent a little time in that area, studying Two Grey Hills weavers, but I haven't been to the trading post at Toadlena for years. Thanks for the tip."

"Let me know if I can be of any further help." Ricardo says. "I'd like to have a copy of those photos. There's something bugging me about the design, but I just can't put my finger on it."

They part and Armida returns to her office, and finds a message from Miguel asking to give him a call at the Albuquerque gallery. She calls, "I need to tell you what I've found out from Ricardo Flores, how's your schedule this week?"

"Open for you, completely open. What do you have in mind?"

"Well, if I can make the arrangements, I'd like to go up into the Two Grey Hills country. I could tell you all about it at supper."

"Sounds great to me," he tells her. "Why don't we go to Los Tres Amigos? I can meet you there about six-thirty. I've got a little work to do here but I'll be finished by then."

After Armida finishes her work, she hurries to her apartment, checks her email, and takes a quick bath. After a number of trial fits, she selects a black nubby knit tee she feels would show off her new hummingbird concha belt and a matching cotton/rayon blend broomstick skirt. Her hummingbird earrings and squash necklace are just the right touch. Armida realizes she is once again dressing for a man.

Since Jose's death, she hasn't paid much attention to her wardrobe. Now, as she looks in her closet, she realizes she probably needed to go shopping, especially for lingerie.

Armida arrives at Los Tres Amigos to find Miguel waiting, handsome as always and dressed in a light blue western cut suit. A matched set of heavy Navajo spider-web turquoise, watch, bolo and belt buckle accent the suit. They order the specialty of the house, gazpacho soup served with quesadillas, and carne asada, a grilled steak. The chef stops by to say hello to Armida and present the couple with a complimentary bottle of Valenzuela wine. She introduces him to Miguel and later, over a creamy berry-pecan flan, tells Miguel what Ricardo has suggested. Miguel agrees to his plan and explains to Armida that the new operator of the Toadlena trading post is a man named Aaron Superstein. Taking out his Palm Pilot, he checks for Superstein's phone number and Armida copies it down. After agreeing to make the trip as soon as Armida can make the arrangements, they part.

By Wednesday morning, the trip arrangements, which include the possibility of an overnight stay in Gallup, are complete. Their drive takes them west on I-70, Old Route 66, one hundred-thirty-nine miles to Gallup, where they stop for a lunch of Navajo tacos before turning north on U.S. 666 toward Shiprock. Sixty miles north they turn west at Newcomb and made the short trip to Toadlena. As they travel through this barren land with its dominating, red plateaus and occasional stands of pinon trees and interrupted by deep ravines, Armida finds she can hardly believe anyone could make a living there. She's always amazed that people who live in such a remote, desolate country produce such beautiful weavings.

At the trading post, Aaron Superstein introduces them to Uaroba's grandson Charlie Daytime. He has been waiting for them and after they are introduced, leads them up a well-worn old game trail, through a grove of pinon trees, to a new mobile home. He then directs them out behind the home to an old hogan, its door facing east. There a grizzled old Indian in leggings and a purple velvet shirt sits on a beautiful old Navajo blanket. He sports about twenty pounds of turquoise jewelry and wears his snow-white hair in a long braid to which an Eagle feather is attached with a shoelace. He's bent over, silently etching small figures with a stick in white sand that is evenly spread out on a small cloth in front of him.

"I will speak for Uaroba." Charlie Daytime explains. "Have a seat."

Miguel and Armida sit down cross-legged on the rug in front of the old Singer and Armida asks Charlie to see if the Singer would be willing to look at some photos. After a brief conversation, Charlie asks. "How much do you pay?"

"What does he want?" Replies Miguel.

"Fifty dollars."

After counting the bills, and putting them in his shirt pocket, Charlie Daytime takes the pictures from Miguel and gives them to the old man who studies them with what appears to be growing concern. "How did you come by these?" he asks abruptly in English.

"There are a couple of men who are offering to sell me the weaving in the photos," Miguel explains.

The old man stands up, his wooden expression giving no clue to indicate if he has recognized the designs on the weaving depicted in the photos. After handing the photos back to Charlie Daytime, he speaks. "If you wish to know the true meaning of this weaving, you must first be purified. I will not speak of such things to those who are not cleansed. If your wish is to do so, you must first fast and prepare your body for the sweat lodge."

Miguel looks at Armida for guidance.

"I'm game if you are," she whispers. Charlie Daytime tells them. "Please fast and be here in the morning at nine." when Miguel agrees, Charlie continues, "The sweat lodge will be prepared." And then, without further comment, he turns away and follows the old Singer into his hogan, an ancient, five-sided structure with walls made of wood crossties.

Getting to their feet, Miguel and Armida stand there perplexed. This is not what they expected. Finally, Miguel breaks the silence. "What do you think?"

"I've read a little about the sweat lodge ceremony," Armida tells him. "But I never dreamed I would get the opportunity to attend one."

"My father attended one when I was a little boy," Miguel tells her as they start back down the trail toward the trading post. "Back then they were illegal. He told me quite a bit about it."

As they stroll along toward the trading post, hand in hand, Armida explains her research indicates that Native spirituality was suppressed by the U.S. government for many years, during which time the sweat lodge ceremony was not condoned. Singers like Uaroba were even threatened with up to thirty years in prison for simply practicing the ritual. Although eventually all this came to an end with the passage of The Freedom of Religion Act in 1978."

The ceremony Navajos like Uaroba practice is classified as the "New Age" type, and requires participants to fast and be nude, both during the ceremony in the lodge, and afterward when they are doused with water outside before being allowed to dress.

The second part of the ceremony usually takes place in a hogan with the smoking of a peace pipe. Since Uaroba is probably a member of the Native American Church the ceremony might also include the use of Peyote as a sacrament. Armida continues to explain that although the use of peyote, a cactus with psychedelic properties, is somewhat protected by the U.S. Constitution and although it is not harmful or habit forming, there is considerable opposition to its use from Christian groups and the government.

"Why the Peyote?" asks a puzzled Miguel.

Armida continues to explain. "Peyote is used in the hogan ceremony to promote visions. It's believed to enable the spirits to occupy the Singer's body during a trance, thus enabling him to traverse the underworld or travel great distances. During the hogan ceremony they might be asked to use peyote. But noted that before they consented to use it they need to understand it's an extremely powerful hallucinogen."

"Do you think we should do this?" asked Miguel.

"Well, the ceremony is probably the only way the old Singer is going to disclose the true meaning of the blanket design. He was disturbed by something he saw in the photos," Armida tells him as they reach the van. "I'm anxious to find out what he knows. I'm not crazy about the nude part, but if that's what it takes, so be it. And you?"

"This is the chance of a lifetime. I'm ready. Let's go for it."

They are quiet during the drive to Gallup as Armida finds herself trying to figure a way to convince her father of her deep feelings for Miguel and Miguel contemplating the ceremony and the answers it might reveal.

When they arrive in Gallup, Armida is relieved to find Miguel has checked them into separate rooms perhaps because things are moving a little faster than she is prepared to handle. Because of their agreement to fast, they skip supper and go straight to their rooms knowing tomorrow would be a challenge for both of them.

CHAPTER 18

Both Armida and Miguel have slept fitfully, perhaps, because they went to bed without eating or because they are close but not together. The next morning they are on their way to the Toadlena trading post and their appointment with Uaroba at 9:00 a.m. Traffic's light and the morning is spectacular. Miguel rose early enough to watch the fiery glow of the sunrise light up the contrail of an overhead jet and as it created a thin pink line across the cloudless New Mexico sky. The temperature, already in the 70's, left little doubt today will be another one hundred-degree plus day.

Last night, on the laptop computer he's never without, Miguel searched the Internet for some additional information on sweat lodge ceremonies. He found out, as he tells Armida the next morning, that, from the ancient times, all over the world, people have participated in ceremonies of cleansing and purification. The biblical accounts of the baptisms performed by John the Baptist referred to them as cleansing ceremonies in which people were 'washed of their sins,' in the Jordon river.

When they arrive, a little early, they're taken by Charlie Daytime to the hogan where he asks that they strip and gives them each a Hudson Bay blanket to use as a robe.

Draped with their blankets, they are escorted a short distance behind the hogan. Among the pinon trees, they see a freshly constructed sweat lodge made from young saplings, its rounded roof covered with an assortment of blankets and a couple of what appear to be old oilcloth tablecloths. Indicating that they remain outside, Charlie lifts the flap and enters the lodge. The wisp of cedar smoke drifts lazily upward from a hole in the center of the roof smells wonderful in the early morning air.

Armida, her blanket wrapped tightly around her, snuggles herself close to Miguel, "Any second thoughts?" she asks.

"A few. I guess. How about you?"

"A little nervous. Hold me."

Miguel takes her in his arms and she clings to him. Just as he's about to kiss her, Charlie comes out of the lodge.

"Uaroba is ready for you," he says, lifting the flap and motioning for them to enter. "Come."

Taking the lead, Miguel bends down to enter the low structure to find Uaroba standing on the other side of a small pile of rocks that rest on a bed of red-hot coals. He's wearing only a G-string flap of leather, a strange, dramatic sight. The right side of his body is painted stark white and the other black. Even his hair has been treated to match his bizarre body coloring. The lodge temperature is oppressively hot. Miguel waits quietly for Armida to follow.

Charlie, now nude himself, follows Armida into the lodge and takes their blankets leaving Armida standing there, naked as the day she was born. In the dim light of the sweat lodge, she's breathtaking to look at. Aroused by being naked in front of two strangers and Miguel, her nipples are erect, and the premature grey streak in her hair seems to capture light from the glowing wood coals. The triangular patch of her profuse dark pubic hair contrasts strikingly against her light brown skin.

Bending down, Uaroba throws a clump of sweet grass on the hot coals and as the smoke drifts upward, he fans little whiffs toward Miguel, motioning for him to turn around, slowly. Miguel does as told and as he turns 360 degrees, the old Singer uses his feather fan to tease the smoke toward every part of Miguel's body. Once this is done, Charlie, who has spread out Miguel's blanket on the floor of the lodge, points for Miguel to be seated.

The old Singer, seemingly detached, repeats the ritual with Armida as she turns slowly in front of him. When she's seated on her blanket next to Miguel, she thinks to herself, 'I can't believe I'm naked in front of three men and yet it feels totally natural.'

Next, Charlie splashes water from a plastic bottle on the rocks, causing a cloud of steam and wood ashes to rise from the hot coals and rocks, raising the temperature as the water vapor quickly humidifies the already hot, humid air. Again, Charlie splashes water on the rocks. Now covered with the grey wood ash and sweating profusely, Miguel glances at Armida and sees the ash has coated her as well. Then Uaroba starts to chant.

For ten minutes he dances, chants, and prays in Navajo while in the corner of the lodge, Charlie sits, cross-legged, thumping on a small drum, occasionally stopping to throw more water on the rocks. Up to this point, although dramatic, the ceremony has little meaning to Miguel or Armida because they speak minimal Navajo.

And then suddenly, Uaroba breaks into English. "This day you come into communication with the Great Spirit. Rather than kneeling with your hands placed side by side in prayer, you have allowed the smoke of sweet grass to be feathered over your entire body for spiritual cleansing. Soon, you will be allowed to smoke from a peace pipe and drift your prayers to the heavens. I am Uaroba and this is how we pray."

Both Miguel and Armida are now sweating heavily. Beads of sweat form and trickle down their bodies, leaving clean streaks as they create a path through the ashes on their skin. The longer they sit there the more drained they felt as the heat and the humidity sap every ounce of their energy.

Then Uaroba stops his dance and shouts, "Hya, Hya, Hya," whereupon the incessant drumbeat stops, and Uaroba turns and leaves the lodge, followed by Charlie. Rising, Armida and Miguel cling together until she gets her legs back.

A little later, guided by Charlie, still wrapped in their blankets, they enter the hogan again to find to Uaroba. His bizarre black and white makeup is now gone, he sits sitting cross-legged on a blanket. The Singer motions for Miguel and Armida to take their place opposite him on another blanket. Between them is a circle of white sand with painted arrows made of blue cornflowers pointing to the four points of a compass. A small fire burns in the center of the circle.

When they are seated, he takes tobacco from a pouch and places a small amount near the little fire, coaxing it into a pile with a single eagle feather. Then he places a pinch of it in a long-stemmed, red, clay peace pipe, which he lights, with a sprig of woven grass after he touches it to the fire. Miguel remembers his father telling him this symbolizes the birth of tobacco. After taking three puffs, Uaroba passes the pipe to Miguel. Miguel takes three puffs and hands the pipe to Armida. As neither Miguel nor Armida smoke, they make no attempt to inhale the harsh, acid tasting smoke from the pipe. The old Singer gets up and using two feather fans coaxes the tobacco smoke upward. Then, apparently satisfied, he sits back down.

From somewhere behind them, Charlie appears, now dressed like Uaroba in a long sleeved red velvet shirt and tan jeans, and sits next to the old Singer. He hands Uaroba a small double spouted, black pot similar to a Santa Clara wedding vase. The old Singer drinks slowly from one spout.

Charlie now becomes their narrator. "The wise one will now take a long journey," he says "Relax. This may take a few minutes." Eyes closed, Uaroba begins rocking back and forth and humming. When he starts to mumble in Navajo, Charlie leans close to him and starts to translate.

"It is a long time ago and it is a bad time. There is fighting and death everywhere. The long coats are afraid. They know our people will no longer tolerate them. They have enslaved us, tortured us, and starved us. But we are strong. We drive them back to their land. We, the Dineh, are the children of the Spider Woman. She protects us. She has said for us to take back what is ours. The Long Coats have taken our sky and hidden it from us. But their tracks are woven in a blanket by one of our women. This sign will lead us to the secret hiding place. You must understand the blanket to find what the Long Coats have hidden from us."

Suddenly, Uaroba crumples over on his side and assumes a fetal position. "He is asleep," Charlie says. "We go now!"

Outside, Charlie says, "Would you care for some breakfast?"

Miguel is quick to reply, "Yes, thank you."

"Please follow me." Orders Charlie.

Up the trail he points to their clothes and clean towels neatly folded on a bench beside a 50-gallon drum of water on which hangs a can for dipping. He then moves on ahead of them. They wash each other as well as they can with the cold water and dress.

Then, following Charlie's path, they arrive at the rear of a manufactured home where a woman, who Charlie introduces as his wife is setting dishes out on a wooden picnic table. Miguel recognizes her immediately. He knows her as Clara Lapahie, one of the finest Burntwater rug weavers on the reservation. Her work is famous and in years past, both he and his father handled her work.

"Clara, I haven't seen you for some time. I had no idea you were here in Toadlena. I lost track of you. How are you? Do you still weave?"

Clara points to a loom, which is barely visible through the window of the home. There is a large, partially woven rug on it. "Clara is one of the finest young weavers I have ever known," Miguel tells Armida. "Her mother was Alfreda Yazzi. Perhaps you have seen her work?"

Armida smiles, "Oh, yes, I know of her mother's work. In fact I've seen examples in several museums."

"When you have eaten, I'll show you the rug I'm working on." Clara says, offering Armida a bowl of warm water and a washcloth.

Breakfast is burritos; green chile scrambled eggs, fresh Indian fry bread and coffee. They are both hungry and the food tastes wonderful. When they're finished, Armida follows Clara into the house.

"It isn't every day we get one of New Mexico's famous Mexican traders here in Toadlena," Charlie offers, as Miguel pours himself another cup of coffee from an old porcelain pot. "I recognized both of you when you came yesterday. I've been to several lectures given by Professor Valenzuela and, of course, some years ago we sold you and your father rugs."

"Why didn't you say something?" Miguel asks.

"I needed to know why you were here." Charlie is now standing, feet apart. "My grandfather's health is failing fast and I wanted to be with him. I was worried you might try to take advantage of him as you have so many of my people. My grandfather is a special man in many ways. If it were not for Navajo Code Talkers like him, many thousands of Americanos would have died in the Great War. He deserves my protection."

Miguel's silent. He's just been insulted and doesn't quite know how to react. Certainly he doesn't consider himself a threat to Uaroba and can't understand why Charlie does.

"I'm on the board of the Crownpoint Rug Weavers Association," Charlie declares. Now he's pacing back and forth, his face flushed. "The government spent a lot of money educating me. I'm a good attorney, and I've done my best to keep traders like you from taking advantage of our people. You pay far too little for our work, Mr. Jaramillo. It's sad because your father was a much fairer man than you. I don't understand why you place so little value on our work when you're buying, and demand a premium price when you sell."

"You're mistaken, Charlie,' Miguel protests. "I've always paid a fair price for your wife and her mother's work."

"Fair by your standard, perhaps. But if you look at how much they are actually paid by the hour, it's less than half of what your government considers minimum hourly wage. Now, when we have a rug to sell, first we try ebay and if it doesn't meet our reserve there, we offer it at Crownpoint. Clara's mother is too old to weave now, so it's only Clara's weaving we have to worry about, but we're determined that her talent is properly valued and not just with lip service but in hard dollars."

I'm sorry you feel that way," Miguel offers. "Obviously there are a lot of things you don't understand about the gallery business."

"Really?" Charlie chides, almost shouting. His face livid with obvious disdain. "Why don't you explain why you stole a valuable old Klagetoh weaving from Desbah Begay in the parking lot of the Crownpoint Auction, even after knowing the weaving was her sister Cora's work and that Cora was dying. She trusted you, and I understand you gave her less than half of what the old rug was worth. One of our board members who knows both Desbah and her sister saw and heard the whole deal go down."

Miguel realizes that he has no come back for Charlie's' indictment. It's true he didn't pay Desbah what the old rug was worth, but she certainly hadn't told him Cora was dying.

"Desbah didn't tell me Cora was about to die," Miguel offers in his own defense.

"Would it have made a difference if she had?" Charlie demands angrily. "Look, you found out today that the old blanket you have photos of may be the key to a lost treasure. A treasure that never belonged to the Spanish. They took it from my forefathers, and it sure as hell doesn't belong to you. If you figure out where the treasure is hidden, it belongs to the Indian Nation. I'm going to be watching. So, if you find it, you better strongly consider turning it over to its rightful owners. If the cache is as valuable as the stories say, it could do a lot of good for my people. So be careful."

Before Miguel can respond, Charlie turns on his heels and strides away. Miguel is standing there mute when Armida comes out of the house with Clara.

The trip back to Albuquerque is a quiet one. Armida's exhausted and before they reach Gallup, she falls asleep in the seat beside Miguel. As for Miguel, Charlie's accusation has been sobering. He has never thought of himself as a bad person. He's simply a sharp trader. His father taught him well. But Charlie's remark about taking advantage of Desbah Begay at Crownpoint hurt the most. He's sure Desbah hadn't told him Cora was dying, and certainly she was under no obligation to accept his offer. But he really didn't know whether his offer would have been different if he had known about Cora.

Miguel's father was always his idol. Everything he did was a reflection of what he thought his father would have approved of. But Charlie said he was not as fair as his father was. As he drives, he tries his best to remember any conversations he'd had with his father about purchase offers. All he can recall were discussions about what various pieces of work should sell for. He can't remember any debates with his father about being fair to the seller. Buying is a game. A highly competitive game, a skilled game about potential profit, not fairness.

But Charlie has struck a cord with his comments about Crownpoint and ebay. Miguel has to admit his supply of quality new rugs has been drying up recently. Perhaps he's been ignoring the signs and kidding himself.

The truth is, although a good many of his father's weavers were still weaving, they no longer offer their rugs to him. At the last Crownpoint Auction, Miguel saw over two hundred buyers in the audience and nearly eighty weavers selling their rugs. Except for the old Klagetoh he purchased from Desbah, he returned home empty handed. The only rug he bid on was the Big

Granada and he recalls it went for $4,450.00. In years past, he and his father bought dozens of comparable Granadas for less than $3,000.00, so Charlie and his Crownpoint Rug Weavers Association are affecting the market price of new Navajo rugs.

Miguel makes a mental note to more frequently check up on Navajo sales activities on ebay. Three years ago, when he first studied ebay auctions on the Internet, very few new Navajo rugs were listed so he paid little attention to them. Lately, he has noticed new Navajo rugs being offered by individual weavers.

So far, he's been fortunate enough to be able to keep a decent inventory of older weavings and rugs in both galleries. But he realizes he's spending a great deal more time each year chasing down old rugs and blankets. Quantity buys like the one he made with the Well's collection in Roswell are very rare

In prior years, he and his father annually made a three-state circuit and visited a wide group of antique stores. The little antique dealers, most of whom were located in small cities and communities, accumulated Navajo rugs during the year and with no local market, would hold onto the weavings, knowing the Jaramillo Gallery would purchase them.

But the steady wholesale supply has dried up since the advent of online auctions. Miguel knows a number of these antique dealers were now offering their weavings directly to customers on ebay and other Internet online auctions. As a matter of fact, this past year, he stopped making the three-state buying trip because there simply weren't enough rugs available to justify the travel. Charlie's more serious charge of not caring about the Native Americans from whom he purchased crafts hurt the most.

Miguel loves New Mexico, its history and its people. If Charlie's charges are true its' a serious matter. His business is dependent on having a regular supply of Indian arts and crafts, and if he is being unfair to the people who make them, he could be in serious trouble.

Even the discovery the design on the old weaving might mark the location of a cache of gold doesn't make up for Charlie's accusations. And Charlie was adamant. The hidden treasure belonged to the Indians. All in all, Miguel Jaramillo has not had a good day.

Armida wakes up as they drive into Albuquerque, and stretches as best she can against her seat belt.

"Where are we?" she asks sleepily.

"On the outskirts of Albuquerque. Did you have a good sleep?"

"Yes, I guess I was out of it. The ceremony really was exhausting. I don't do well without food and I didn't sleep well last night."

"I need a long hot shower and something to eat. How about some supper?" Miguel asks her.

"I agree with the clean up part," she tells him. But I think all I want to do is go to bed."

The events of the day have left her shattered emotionally. The fact that she still has no idea whether or not the ritual they took part in has any significance. And then there is Clara, so tired and worn, because she's' spent a lifetime being forced to create the beauty that people like she and Miguel took for granted.

Later, luxuriating in her bath, Armida can not keep herself from thinking about Clara. She's only thirty-nine years old, but her hands are deformed, damaged irreparably by years of working with dyes and wool, and sitting at her loom pulling the wool threads, she's also stooped when she walks. Clara's condition has brought home to Armida, not for the first time, how difficult weaving is for the Navajo women.

Armida's expertise in Navajo weaving and other Southwest Indian crafts is extensive and every time she's exposed to their lifestyle she ends up feeling deeply sorry for them. More and more she has come to realize how much effort is required to create these beautiful pieces of work and how little money the Navajo weavers receive for their effort.

She feels the same way about the Mexican immigrants who work the land. Armida was raised in a very sheltered environment; the Valenzuelas being part of the remaining fragments of a class hierarchy created during the early stages of the Spanish colonization of New Mexico in the good old days, the days before the *Americanos* came. As a result, in some ways, Armida is ill equipped to take over the rancho and become a wine maker. She knows she will be in charge of field labor, many of whom are recent immigrants. Of course she can rely on her foreman as Carlos had, but she's aware there will be times when she must deal directly with the workers and in rare moments like this, she realizes she needs a mate who relates to people and is a good business man. A man like Miguel. She lies there in the hot soapy water and thinks about what life could be with him.

CHAPTER 19

Thursday morning Armida signs for the Federal Express package sent by Ricardo Flores' friend at Red Rock. After opening it, she finds a D.N.A. swab sample taken from Narbona's great grandson. Hurrying down to the lab, she asks that a comparison between the swab and the D.N.A. found in the blood sample taken from the old blanket be obtained as soon as possible.

The day before, her father was in town for a meeting with local law enforcement officials to assure himself that the person responsible for the attack on Mary and the break-ins would be prosecuted. Armida and her father had enjoyed a leisurely lunch during which her father brought up Miguel, asking a number of questions about him, some of which she was unable to answer. But it was a relief to her that at least her father seemed willing to discuss Miguel. For the first time she thought he might actually have an understanding of her feelings toward this Latino, at least he seemed to be trying.

Armida's plans call for some cataloging today, but all that changes when Ricardo calls. "Buenõs Dias, Armida."

"Buenõs Dias," Ricardo, thank you for the D.N.A. sample."

"You're welcome. I called to tell you I've discovered what's been bugging me about those pictures of the weaving with the crazy designs on it. I've done some research and I'd like to share my findings with you."

"Fine. Can you come to my office?"

"I'll be right there," he replies.

After sitting down at Armida's desk, he removes a manila folder out of his briefcase and takes out a copy of a line drawing. "This drove me crazy until I finally remembered where I saw the design." He hands it to Armida. "Do you recognize this?"

Armida studies the image on the paper for a few moments. "You're right. There are differences to be sure, but the two are amazingly similar."

"It's a site map I drew of the location of structures at Gran Quivira, a Seventeenth Century Jumano Pueblo located a few miles south of Mountainair." Ricardo offers. "I visited there a few years ago. I'm surprised I didn't recognize the layout right away. On the weaving, the larger rectangle is the site of the Chapel of San Isidro. The circles are the Kivas. The connected squares represent the rooms in the living quarters. I think the small X's are the locations of the cisterns. The larger X is not on any of the site maps I could locate, but I have an idea what it depicts."

Armida can't believe what she's hearing. She looks at the drawing again. "Please continue."

"Well, let me share what I've discovered so far, I think you will find it fascinating." Ricardo says, sitting back in his chair. "Gran Quivira is probably one of the most famous of the treasure sites in New Mexico. For years there have been persistent rumors of a treasure trove located there in Spanish times. Most of the digging at Gran Quivira has been done within the walls of the San Isidro church. The small church structure is represented by the rectangle in the design.

How such a bleak and poverty ridden site, in a country so poor in minerals, and the sub-surface wealth restricted to scanty supplies of unpotable water, came to be associated with rich treasure, is something for conjecture."

"I've been near there but not at the Gran Quivira site," replies Armida.

"Well as near as I can determine, the tales of riches are based on the supposition that about the time of abandonment, around 1680, the Spaniards buried either valuable gold bells or an accumulated treasure from mining operations there for safe keeping."

Armida listens intently as Ricardo explains the stories of the treasure appear to have originated with the survivors of the abandonment of 1692, since there are references, about a century later, to buried treasure at the site. By the mid 1800's there's evidence of multiple attempts of indefatigable treasure hunters at the site.

One particular treasure hunt at Gran Quivira was started in the 1780's by the Don Pablo Yrisarri family and continued until 1933, and ended inside the church of San Isidro. It was thought the family passed the secret from father to a son and that a grandson was reported to be digging within the walls of the church, following a map scratched on a white stone found by the grandfather.

His digging was interrupted, and he was taken to Santa Fe and fined for violating the Antiquities Act. When the area became a national monument and unauthorized mining became illegal, treasure seekers took recourse in permits."

"They grant very few permits of that type now days," comments Armida.

Ricardo goes on. "You're right, the last permit was issued in November of 1930 and allowed for excavation of certain buried treasure alleged to be concealed in government property at Gran Quivira. Jacob Yrisarri showed up again to undertake the work. Jacob started in the apse of San Isidro and appeared to be following two lines of evidence to the treasure written on a white stone unearthed by his grandfather. Following the map on the white stone, he interpreted it to indicate the shaft should be first sunk in the San Isidro. From this shaft a tunnel would be found running northwest where it intersected a second tunnel running to a treasure cellar at the foot of a hill."

"Yrisarri began work on September 17, 1932, with a force of ten men, later reduced to three. He reached a depth of 40 feet and began tunneling eastward. He encountered solid rock at the 42-foot level and dug a tunnel 23 feet long in an eastern direction. The walls beyond the timbered area resembled those found in Carlsbad Caverns and there was a fairly strong current of fresh air in the crevice, indicating small caverns or rooms might lie ahead. The tunnel, or cleaned crevice, was extended to 36 feet, 4 feet short of his projected interception with the other tunnel."

"For some reason, work stopped at this point. The permit expired in

December of 1933. In 1934 Yrisarri attempted to have it extended but he was denied. In 1940 the shaft was back-filled and the work obliterated as much as possible though continued settling has revealed the spot. No further permits have been granted." Ricardo sits back and takes a deep breath.

"When you research something, you do a thorough job," Armida ventures, smiling.

Again Ricardo drones on. "A number of the Jumanos Indians who inhabited the Gran Quivira pueblo headed north to the Rio Grande valley after abandonment and intermixed with residents there. At the same time, as you are probably aware, there were Navajo women living within the Pueblos in the lower Rio Grande. Some were ex-slaves of the Spanish and some were there because of intermarriage. Perhaps one of the Jumanos told of the treasure and the location ended up as part of the weaving, or perhaps the Jumano was also a slave and his or her owner ordered the weaving. It's a likely possibility. What do you think?"

"Miguel and I visited Uaroba as you suggested," Armida tells him. "And I must tell you that he said this was indeed a treasure map. He claimed not to know the location. But I'm not so sure. He acted like he knew what he was looking at and insisted we go through the sweat lodge ceremony. The strange thing is, if the treasure's location was such a secret, why would it be worked into a weaving? It might make more sense to think one of the Spaniards, perhaps a priest, had the weaving done as a personal record of a gold stash. Maybe the symbol of the "Long Coats" in the corner indicates their involvement."

"That could be." Ricardo agrees. "I've had a blast researching this. I love this state. There's so much history I have yet to discover. It's a never-ending challenge. Now I have another story to tell in my lectures." Ricardo closes his brief case and rises from his chair. "I'd love to have a chance at going after the treasure with you."

Armida gets out of her chair and gives him a hug.

"You're a jewel for looking all this up. You've certainly earned the right to go with us. But I have a feeling this isn't going to be an easy task. It's not that simple to obtain a permit to treasure hunt on a national monument site.

CHAPTER 20

As Armida drives into the lot in the rear of the Jaramillo Gallery, she's pleasantly surprised to find her name on a newly painted sign in a parking space. Parking space in the Historic Old Town Plaza area of Albuquerque is almost nonexistent at this time of the year, as thousands of tourists jam into the area. Miguel suggested they have lunch at a popular restaurant, the Hacienda, and when Armida expressed some hesitancy because of difficulty of finding a parking place, he told her to just pull in behind his gallery. Now she knew why. This consideration for her was one of the special things about him. How pleasant it is to have someone care for her.

As she enters through the back door, she sees Miguel, with a clipboard in his hand, taking inventory.

"See you use it often," Miguel says, giving her a quick kiss, after she thanks him for the reserve spot. She returns his kiss with a passion that surprises him and wanting more, they kiss deeply.

"Miss me?" asks Armida.

"More than you know," he says holding her face in his hands, "*Te amo, Mi Amor.*"

"*Y yo Te amo, Mi Corazon.*"

The Hacienda, famous for cooking sopaipillas and tortilla chips right in the middle of the serving area is located one block from the Jaramillo Gallery. The old restaurant features several large trees growing right out of the floor and up through glass skylights in the main dinning room. Today, however, they decide to be seated in the exterior patio section. After they order, Armida leans toward Miguel. "I have a surprise for you," she says in a low voice.

"Really? What is it?"

"I believe Ricardo has figured out the location of the gold cache depicted on the old weaving.

He brought me this." And with that, she hands him a copy of the site plan, indicating the location of the foundations of the Gran Quivira monument ruins and one of the photos of the old weaving.

"I believe he's right," Miguel says after studying the site plan and the photo for what seems like an eternity.

"The more I look them over the more I agree with his conclusion."

"I'd like to go see the site," Armida says unable to contain her excitement. "It's only about a three-hour drive."

"It's south of Mountainair, isn't it?"

"Yes, I called and it's open Monday through Saturday. There's quite a bit of information available. I'm studying up. What do you think?"

"I'm afraid the next couple of weeks are out for me," Miguel tells. The Annual Indian Market starts Monday and I'm up to my ears until it's over."

Armida reflects. "I may have a problem too. Our grape harvest should start about a week after the Indian Market. We put ours up a little earlier because of the temperate. The harvests from the southern vineyards are later, due to their longer growing season. Well, we'll just have to see when we can get together to go. Let me fill you in on what Ricardo found out."

For the balance of their lunch, Miguel listens intently as Armida relays the information Ricardo shared with her about Gran Quivira. The information is particularly interesting since they are both aware that most tales about the Spanish gold quest in the Southwest centered on the Spaniard's belief in the mythical Seven Cites of Gold.

"The Spanish believed the cities were located somewhere far north of Mexico City. Who started the story of the Seven Cities of Gold, also known as the Seven Cities of Cibola, is not known. It's a matter of record that the Spanish, since the time of the Conquistadors, were all, in one way or another, involved in the search for gold and these illusive seven cities, there are dozens of references and information on expeditions coming Northward from Mexico in search of gold."

Miguel offers, "One of my artists has created a life-size bronze of the most famous of these guys. A conquistador named Francisco Vasquez Coronado. He claims that historians think Francisco is the one who made the most meaningful discovery and exploration of this land. And he is generally accepted as the one who set the stage for Spain's claim to what is now known as the southwestern part of the States. But all he found was stone and adobe buildings, no gold. Even though he sent out numerous scouting parties who chased rumors and investigated a large section of New Mexico and Western Texas. His dreams of treasure never came true. In 1542 he returned to Mexico a beaten man. Today, the stories of buried treasure still persist however, but no one has found it. It's fascinating that we may have stumbled upon what he missed."

Over coffee they discuss Miguel's expectations for the Indian Market and the latest developments on the D.N.A. test on the old Narbona wearing blanket. Armida tells him she should have the results back in the week and agrees to let him know the results as soon she receives them.

After lunch she stops by a couple shops and picks up some new lingerie. It's nearly three by the time she gets back to the museum, arriving just in time to sign for a certified envelope from the D.N.A. testing laboratory. With so much at stake, she hesitates to open the report. She puts the folder, unopened, on the corner of her desk and checks her telephone messages. Then she looks over the test results on three of the new weavings acquired in a six-piece trade with an Arizona museum. The trade resulted in her museum gaining a better representation of Rio Grande Blankets in exchange for some duplicates and surplus transitional pieces. At last, unable to resist looking at the D.N.A. results any longer, she retrieves the envelope and opens it. The report indicates there's a problem with the results due to the age of the blood sample and it is being forwarded to another lab for further testing. Disappointed by what she reads, Armida can't help but wonder if the old blanket is really Narbona's, and decides to request another D.N.A. sample from Ricardo's friend. Perhaps this one will be less contaminated.

CHAPTER 21

Carlos Valenzuela is about fifty yards from the grape processing shed when the pain hits, a sharp searing pain that takes his breath away. Then suddenly his chest feels like someone is standing on it, and he breaks out in a heavy sweat. He's never felt anything quite like this before but knows instantly he's having a heart attack. When momentarily, the pain diminishes, he crumples to the ground clutching his chest. As he fades in and out of consciousness, he dimly sees Juan, the vineyard foreman, bending over him.

Outside Carlos's hospital room, the doctor, Henri Alto, is assuring Armida her father is in good hands, explaining that the preliminary tests indicate Carlos indeed has suffered a heart attack. He goes on to tell her he's scheduling her father for an angiogram at seven the next morning, at which time he will be able to tell her more about his condition. In the meantime, there's a video they can watch that will explain the procedure.

It's obvious that Carlos likes the doctor and Armida is relieved. Watching the angiogram video together, Armida and Carlos see the procedure involves the insertion of a special catheter into an artery in the groin from which it is manipulated upward, through the artery to the patient's heart. The doctor then introduces x-ray dye and watches on a fluoroscope as the dye flows through the arteries and veins in the heart. The procedure allows the doctor to detect any blockage and determine if further procedures are called for.

The hard part for Carlos will come after the instruments are removed since he will be required to lie there perfectly still, flat on his back for several hours with pressure pads on the area in the groin where the equipment entered his artery.

After the video, Carlos dozes off because of the medication the doctor prescribed. Armida comforts him and stays with him for an hour, until visiting hours are over.

Later, alone in his room, Carlos awakens, suddenly, frightened. Although he has never participated in any sport, he has exercised regularly and always considered himself fit. Now he realizes his heart might have failed him and it's very difficult to accept. The aging process is a subtle one to men like Carlos, and it's a shock when they have to face their own mortality.

Carlos lies there taking stock of his life. He knows it's time for him to make some serious decisions. He isn't blind; his only child is obviously in love with that Latino. He hoped she would marry a Castilian, but now that's fast becoming a remote possibility and he's forced to struggle once again with the realization that the Valenzuela family name may soon no longer be associated with his family's heritage. Of course, with no son, the name change has always been inevitable but Jaramillo is not even a Castilian name. He's not sure he's willing to accept a Latino as a son-in-law.

However, Carlos is aware his immediate problem is what his tests might show in the morning and right now that's worry enough.

Back in her apartment, the reality of what has happened to her father is setting in, and Armida can't help but wonder if she was partially to blame for his attack. She knows he has been very upset at her announcement that she is in love with Miguel. On previous occasions, when the subject of her marrying outside the Castilian family came up, her father made it clear how opposed he was to such possibility.

She understands why he feels this way, but Miguel has awakened feelings she thought she might never again experience.

The years since Jose's death have been busy ones but lonely ones. Miguel has many qualities that are not common in Castilian men. He's thoughtful, gentle and caring. The more she's with him, the more she realizes she must find a way to convince Carlos that Miguel is the right man for her.

She calls Miguel, only to begin sobbing when he answers the phone. When she finally gains control, she tells him what has happened. Miguel tells her he's about twenty-five miles north of Albuquerque and he will be at her condo within the hour.

When Armida answers her door, she falls into Miguel's arms. He holds her for a long time and tries to comfort her. She finally quiets down and they make plans for meeting at the hospital in the morning. Before leaving they kiss and Miguel again holds her.

The next day, she and Miguel spend the morning in the waiting room, while Carlos lies recovering from the angiogram procedure. At last Doctor Alto comes out.

"Our tests indicate your Father has blockage in two arteries, enough to be borderline, but at this time I am not recommending any invasive surgical procedure. I'm going to prescribe a beta-blocker, a cholesterol lowering drug, and one aspirin every day. He'll have to exercise. Walking would be the best. He'll also need to watch his diet and avoid stressful situations. If he behaves himself, he should recover nicely but I impressed upon him that he would have to accept a new life style. If he doesn't, we'll have him right back here in the hospital."

With a sigh of relief, Armida thanks the doctor and hugs Miguel before they go up to Carlos' room.

When they enter, they found Carlos hooked up to some monitoring equipment looking pale and drawn.

Carlos greets them weakly.

"How are you doing?" Armida asks him, taking his hand.

"They had a bit of a problem and I bled a little," he says. "I'm black and blue but otherwise I'm doing fine. Although I still feel like I'm doped up. I'm worried about the grapes. Juan's never had to handle a harvest by himself. They're about ready to harvest. If the weather holds, next week we should start. That damn fool doctor said it would not be wise for me to run the harvest. That's like me telling him to stop his practice."

"Don't worry, Papa. I've got plenty of vacation time, and I'll take care of the harvest."

"I don't know how much help I'll be."

"Papa I don't need your help. I'll be fine. This isn't my first harvest, you know. All you have to do is bring me up to date and I'll handle it."

"I know, I know. But it's hard to step aside. The doctor tells me I have to change my life style. We need to talk."

"Papa, there's plenty of time for talk. Right now you need to rest. I'll get things squared away at the University, and take you back to the rancho tomorrow."

Noticing that Carlos is dozing off again she gives him a hug and a kiss. Miguel wishes him well and they leave. Outside the hospital Miguel asks, "What can I do to help?"

"Love me. I need your support. I need you."

"Not a problem. Anything you need, any time. Please ask."

They part and Armida heads for the University, wondering what to do, she has so way to many problems to think about. Miguel, her father, the grape harvest and what this all will mean to her full time job at the university. The only thing she knows for sure is that her life is about to change drastically. Too many problems to think about today. She has to get organized.

CHAPTER 22

Miguel is not particularly pleased that he has been forced to take some time from his busiest season to give a deposition for the Reyes brother's arraignment in federal court. Since he didn't realize he would be needed as a witness against Tomas and Jacinto Reyes, the call from the police came as a bit of a surprise. He really doesn't think he can offer anything new. All he can say is how he obtained the piece of the old weaving and confirm the brothers offer to sell him the rest of the fabric. But the prosecutor wants him there, and so he agrees. Armida called and told him she was also needed, so here they are sitting in the back of an Albuquerque Federal courtroom waiting for the proceedings to start.

The brothers are being charged with violation of the Antiquities Act of 1906. In addition they are in violation of the 1990 Native American Graves and Repatriation Act (NAGPRA), an act that assigns ownership and control of American cultural items, human remains, and associated funerary objects to Native Americans. It also establishes requirements for the treatment of sacred or cultural objects found or taken from Federal lands, thereby giving Native Americans the power to decide what happens to such items. Among the Native American lawyers present in the courtroom is Charlie Daytime who acknowledges Miguel with a nod.

A search warrant for the homes and warehouse of the Reyes' brothers has yielded a large cache of pottery, tools, artifacts and sacred items that the Reyes brothers obviously have no right of ownership. There appears to be no question the Reyes brothers have been dealing in illegal antiquities, but its' necessary for the items to be declared as antiquities. To qualify as an antiquity, the items must be at least 100 years old. Armida's testimony is needed to authenticate the age of the weaving sample and other recovered items.

Apparently, among the numerous sites the brothers excavated, in the Canyon de Muerto area, was a cave, which was used for burial purposes. There they discovered a large cache of goods. Armida thinks that is where the old weaving came from. Everything the investigators found was confiscated and now if the federal prosecutor is successful, the Reyes brothers will be held over for trail. The Native American lawyers are there to monitor the disposition of the found items.

One by one, the officers who participated in the search of the Reyes' residences and warehouse identify the numerous items they discovered. The quantity of goods described in the charges makes this one of the largest recent hauls of illegal Indian artifacts, and has created headlines all over the country. Dozens of reporters and three TV crews cover the proceedings and Miguel and Armida had found themselves besieged as they entered the courthouse.

After about two hours of presentations, Armida and several other experts are called on to verify the age and origin of the items. As the last witness called to the stand, Miguel relates how he obtained the scrap of the weaving. He then verifies the Reyes brothers offered to sell him the entire weaving. The prosecution shows him photos of the scarp and asks him to identify the weaving scrap and the photos that the brothers gave him when they were trying to sell him the whole weaving.

At a lunch break Miguel and Armida go to a nearby restaurant. "How's the harvest going?" Miguel asks after they order.

"Very well," she says. "Almost all the grapes are in, and we're processing ours. We're keeping about 20 percent of the crop. The balance has been purchased by the Jemes Winery in Taos. We don't have the equipment or manpower to put up much more than that. Some day I'm hoping we can expand and use our entire crop, but I'm not sure we ever will."

"You look tired." Miguel offers.

"I am a little, but we start processing now. It's meticulous, but doesn't take a lot of energy. I haven't been sleeping that well."

"Who's been covering at the museum?"

"There are several assistant curators. The place is in good hands. They're preparing the weavings for my upcoming show. I'm sure they will do an excellent job. I still haven't received the final D.N.A. report back on the Narbona blanket. The first one wasn't conclusive and I've submitted a second blood sample for testing. I plan on featuring it on the cover, if the D.N.A. proves it was Narbona's. Thanks again for letting us display it. Have you made up your mind what you are going to do with it?"

"I haven't made a firm decision yet. I'll let you know as soon as I make a final decision."

"Well, you know how much it would mean for it to be in the museum's collection. I hope you give us serious consideration."

"Of course I will. But I'm still considering a couple of other options."

The rest of the lunch is devoted to a discussion about Carlo's health and the vineyard. Armida perks up as she relates the details of her harvest.

After lunch, they return to the courtroom and after a couple more presentations, the judge makes his decision to hold the Reyes brothers over for trial. Bail is set at $250,000.00.

Because Armando has pleaded guilty, he too appears as a witness for the prosecution. He looks very tired and frail and seeks out Armida to apologize for hurting Mary and ransacking her apartment. Armida accepts his apology. She has been told when the Reyes trial is over Armando will be sentenced for assault.

Outside the courtroom, Armida and Miguel make plans for their trip to Gran Quivira and agree to include Ricardo Flores. They have no intention of taking anything they find at Gran Quivira as their own property. Their investigation will be conducted under the auspicious of the museum, and they decide any materials discovered will be given to the Government for disposition.

Armida promises to put her father to work politically to obtain permission to dig at the site. Not an easy job, but one she knows he will jump at it, no matter how difficult. He does love to use his influence. The thrill of the treasure hunt excites them. Miguel asks if Armida is staying over, but she says she really needs to get back to the rancho.

Back at the rancho, Armida is at the computer in the laboratory in the shed when Carlos comes in. "I'm working on the manifests," she says, looking up. "It looks like a great crop, a banner year."

"I'm sorry that I can't be of more help. I'm sure it's the medicine they're making me take. I'm going back to see if there is something else they can give me."

"Don't worry. We got by fine. I'm sure you'll feel better soon. We had a good crew and got the grapes in. Now it's only processing and waiting to see how good the vintage is."

"Mu*chacha*, you look tired," Carlos worries aloud. Armida responds,

"Oh, I was doing fine until I went to Albuquerque for that trial. I need a little rest then I'll be fine."

"There's something I want to tell you," her father says in a serious tone. "I watched you handle the harvest, and I'm proud of you. You did a great job. I've underestimated you. I've decided to turn over the vineyard and winery to you. It's time. What do you say?"

Armida's mind is spinning. She can't believe what she's hearing. Ever since she was a teenager, she has wanted to work full time in the vineyard and she loves making wine.

With today's challenges in viticulture, and so much to be learned about new strains of grapes, she knows she will never tire of wine making. Northern New Mexico is an ideal location to raise the finest of the newer French/American hybrids, and Carlos has chosen to plant only two varieties. At the Valenzuela rancho she feels the shallow sandy loam and the rancho's higher elevation will allow these new varieties to thrive. She's the one who wants to try some other varieties, but Carlos has resisted. Now, Carlos offering her the chance to make decisions and go for her dream.

"Oh, Papa." She gets up from the computer and runs to his arms. "I love you, I've always wanted to work with the grapes. Of course I'll do it."

"You deserve the chance," he tells her. "I'll get our attorney to handle the paper work. I've decided to give you a credit line of a million dollars to modernize and expand the business."

"Papa, I have so many ideas and I can hardly wait to get started," Armida says. Her eyes are dancing and she can hardly contain her excitement. "First I'll have to inform the university. There are three assistant curators who will jump at the chance to take my place. I have one show left in October that I'd like to do. I'll give them ninety days notice and that will let me finish on a high note. I've worked two years putting this display of early weavings together."

"I'm sure it will all work out. You can stay here at the hacienda or maybe we should think about building a new casa for you. Whatever you wish.

You'll need to keep your wits about you and not be affected by outside influences. This is a big responsibility," he adds ominously.

"I'll stay here with you. I'd like to hire Mary when we get going. I think she would be excellent in the lab and winery. Then you could have Jesse around all the time." Mary is recovering nicely and has been able to spend a few hours in the vineyard lab, assisting with the tests and identification. And Jesse is constantly at Carlos' side when Juanita isn't tutoring him.

"I'd like that. I plan on spending more time in the stables. I may get a few more mares and put Golden Boy to work."

"Papa, you've got a lot to teach me." Armida says, now very serious, and paces back and forth as the ramifications of taking over the vineyard sober her. "There is so much I don't know."

"I've watched you the last three weeks and I think you know a lot more than you give yourself credit for. You'll be fine. But I'll be here to help when you need me."

Off and on the rest of the day, Armida and her father discuss various aspects of her taking over the vineyard. At last, weary from the day's events she goes to bed, resisting the temptation to call Miguel. Tomorrow will be soon enough. She can hardly wait, but something her father said pesters her. What had he meant by outside influences?

CHAPTER 23

The Indian Market is over. It's been a successful one for Miguel. Attendance was up, and buyers were plentiful. Every year Miguel looks forward to the occasion with some degree of concern since such a large amount of his Santa Fe gallery's annual sales are dependent upon it. But, as it turns out, this year he needn't have been concerned since he experienced the highest sales week in his Santa Fe gallery's history. It was the inventory from the Well's collection that made the difference. At times it seemed that as fast as he pulled a Well weaving out of the vault, there was a buyer waiting. The prices he received were also higher than he had anticipated.

For some reason, a large number of interior decorators seemed to have money to spend, and Miguel got more than his share. The general public was more interested in modern Zuni or Navajo jewelry, but to his surprise, even basket and pottery sales were good. The only slow area was original art. Sluggish sales of bronzes and paintings didn't particularly surprise him since this was the trend for the last two years, partially because of Miguel's refusal to sell prints of any kind in his galleries. Like his father, he considered them calendar art and long ago decided if he had to stoop to selling colored pictures from a printing press on paper as an art form, he would find another business.

The past week, every time he had a moment to himself, Armida was on his mind. Thinking of her is a new and exciting experience and Miguel's amazed at how easily he recalls everything about her. Her smell. Her lithe body, like that of a runner. The way she walks like a runway model, hips swaying. The skill and the ferocity of the passion with which she makes love takes his breath away. Even her habit of greeting him in Spanish, fascinates him. He has never known a woman as totally captivating as Armida.

There have been times when he'd almost given up finding a mate, but now there is no question in his mind that he has found a beautiful, captivating woman with whom he wants to spend the rest of his days. He has called daily to inquire of her progress and Carlos' recovery. Today when he calls Armida answers with a lift in her voice.

"You caught me working on the daily weight tickets this morning. We're about to wrap it up and it looks like we're going to have a great harvest. Our quality is fabulous, and we're getting top dollar for our surplus grapes."

"That's great. How's Carlos today?"

"I think he's a little better, but he doesn't have much energy. It could be his medication. He's been unable to spend time with the pickers, so this morning I have him weighing and checking the transport trucks."

"I'm glad to hear he's doing better," Miguel says.

"How are you holding up?"

"Great. I'm actually amazed at how much I know. I guess I'm a good learner. The hours are long, but so far no problems. When can you come up and see our operation?"

"Any time. The Market is over and sales were wonderful. Things are calming down here so you make the call, and I'll be there."

"We're actually running seven days a week until we finish processing the grapes, so come any time. I have some great news and I'll take a break to show you how we do our thing."

"I'll be up late in the morning tomorrow if that's all right. Can I bring you anything?"

"You're all I want."

"I'll be there. *Te amo*, Armida."

"*Yo Te amo, mi amante*."

Now Miguel is faced with a real dilemma. He's made up his mind he wants to marry Armida, but now with Carlos' heart problems he can't be sure his timing is right. He's worried himself sick about how to approach the old patron.

Carlos is a proud man and even prouder of his Spanish heritage. Miguel understands he must treat him respectfully but decides he can delay the talk no longer.

If the opportunity presents itself tomorrow, he's going to risk asking for Armida's hand in marriage. Taking the ring he's purchased from the safe, he puts it in his briefcase. He recognizes the risk he's taking, but he feels sure of Armida's feelings for him. All he can do is hope Carlos will approve of him.

The next morning, he's on the road to the Valenzuela rancho, planning what he wants to say to Carlos. He calls ahead and Armida is waiting in front of the hacienda as he pulls up. She's dressed in tan, bib style, grape stained overalls, her hair in a pony tail, even so, looking as beautiful as she ever has as far as Miguel's concerned.

"Miss me?" she whispers, as she steps close and gives him a kiss.

"You know I did. Every minute."

"Good, come in. We're having a bite to eat."

Lunch, is being served on the patio with its oversize white wicker table and chairs. Lunch is of broiled chicken, grilled yam flautas and a red wine. The conversation is devoted to an update on the harvest. Carlos, who looks his old self, seems satisfied with the price they are receiving for their surplus grapes, but distressed at the cost of the field hands. His attitude toward Miguel seems friendly enough.

When they finish lunch Armida suggests she and Miguel take a quick tour. "Papa, we'll meet you at the scale when we're finished."

"*Bueno, muchacha*. Take your time."

In the distance Miguel can see thirty or so workers finishing up the grape harvest. He and Armida ride in a golf cart to one of the locations where the last of the pickers are working. There, she shows him how the bunches were being removed from the vine with a short curved knife. "Would you like to try a little picking?"

"This could get old fast." Miguel tells her after a few minutes of removing grapes.

Armida laughs and says, "Wait till you've been at it all day and you'll see how old it gets. Come on I've got something to show you."

They go back to the golf cart and she drives to a long shed nestled against a red, sandstone bluff. Carlos is outside weighing a truck loaded with grapes. Inside the first room, the crews are cleaning grape pulp from a big machine while in another; fresh barrels are being rolled into storage.

In the little lab, Armida shows Miguel how they test and identify each batch of grapes for blending at a later date. As she explains the blending process, he realizes she's in her element, passionate and radiant. Then, without warning, she closes the blinds on the windows and locks the door. Turning back to Miguel, she says,

"Come over here."

He moves close and she kisses him passionately, her tongue exploring his mouth. The next thing he knows she has slipped off the straps of her overalls and is guiding his hands to her breasts.

"I've missed you. She murmurs. "I want you in me, now."

Miguel kisses her neck and throat as she lets her coveralls drop to the floor and steps out of her panties. Next she unbuckles his belt, reaches in, and frees his already swollen manhood. Then leaning back against her desk she spreads her legs, and he finds her clearly wet and ready. Miguel enters her easily, and hears her purr as she responds to his every thrust. As she undulates through a series of orgasms, her purrs turn to cries of sheer pleasure. This is urgent, raw, intense sex and when he comes, she whispered, "See, you needed me, and God knows I needed you. I can't get enough of you *mi amante*," she tells him when it's over.

"I love you," Miguel says, "like I've never loved anyone before."

"I'm yours anytime you want me. *Mi Amor*," I've got something to tell you. Papa's told me he's going to turn over the vineyard to me." As she dresses she's beaming and tells him of her plans and how she was completely taken by surprise at his decision.

"That's wonderful," replies Miguel, "I'm thrilled for you. I know how much this means to you. I'm sure you will be great at running the vineyard and will make your dreams come true."

Armida's once again in his arms and they hold each other for a long time. Armida removes herself from Miguel's arms. "I've got a couple things to get straightened out with my foreman. Why don't we go and find Papa."

Outside the shed, the truck has left, and Carlos sits at a table under an umbrella. "How did you like your tour?" he asks.

"It was fascinating. This is a busy place," Miguel replies, hoping Carlos hasn't noticed Armida's flushed face. "The harvest looks like it's going well."

While Armida speaks with her foreman, Miguel takes a seat next to Carlos. After they chat about the winery for a few minutes, Miguel decides to put his cards on the table.

"Carlos," he says. "Armida told me of your decision to turn the vineyard over to her, and I'm thrilled for her. I'd like to bring up something else for your consideration. I'd like your permission to speak with Armida about marriage. My hope is she will honor me by becoming my wife."

He sits back and waits while Carlos casually removes a cigar from a silver container, which he carries in his pocket. "I'm not supposed to be smoking these," he says, offering one to Miguel.

Miguel declines. "No thanks I've quit."

From the moment Armida has revealed her love for Miguel, Carlos has anticipated this proposal, even though this is one more problem he doesn't' need right now. As a matter of fact it's one of the reasons he's made his decision to turn over the vineyard to Armida at this time. But he also knows he must be realistic. He's well aware his breed is a dying breed in New Mexico and he also knows the Valenzuela family's future depends upon business decisions made by those of Armida's generation. She has waited almost too long to find a new man. But Carlos prefers a Castilian man. Although he knows Miguel, like his father, is a keen businessman, he isn't sure he wants him running the Valenzuela wine business.

Viticulture is the future of the Valenzuela rancho and Armida the key. She knows how to raise grapes and make wine but lacks experience in marketing. He knows Miguel is a salesman, a damned good one and would probably be an asset to her operation. But he just can't abide her marrying a Latino. In quiet but firm voice he says, "Amigo, I'm not sure I can give such permission at this time."

Miguel's thunder struck. He's well aware that Carlos might have some reservations about his proposal, but he has just heard a distinct turn down. He is disheartened and deeply disappointed but decides to press the issue.

"I've never asked a woman to marry me. Armida will be the first. She has every quality I hoped to find in a wife. I love her and I'm sure she loves me."

Carlos looks straight at Miguel and says in a firm voice. "You have my answer for now. I need more time to consider this. I will speak with Armida but she has a lot to deal with right now. You should respect my concern. Armida is my only child. This is a critical time for her." With that he pauses and takes a long draw on his cigar.

Miguel sits there in silence. He really hadn't expected Carlos' rejection. This is a nightmare, one he is not prepared for and he finds himself at a loss for words. He's about to make another plea, when Armida walks up and thinking better of it he turns toward her.

"Armida, I believe its time for me to leave. I must get back to Santa Fe."

It's obvious to Armida that something has happened between her father and Miguel. They get into the golf cart and head for Miguel's van. Miguel's very quiet until they reach his van. "Armida, I asked your father for you hand in marriage and he did not give it."

"What?" Shouts Armida. "What did he say?"

"He said he could not give his permission, adding that he needed more time to consider my request."

"Well, my answer is yes. I don't care what Papa said."
With that, she takes Miguel's face in both hands and kisses him again and again.

"I love you and want to be your wife." Then she begins to cry.

Miguel holds her tight, trying to comfort her as she sobs. Finally she quiets down and steps away.

"I'll handle Papa. You've just made me the happiest woman in the world and I'm not about to let him spoil this moment. I love you and there's nothing he can do to stop my becoming your wife."

The trip back to Santa Fe is not a happy one for Miguel. Armida's engagement ring is still in his pocket. It should have been on her finger. In all the confusion, he failed to offer it to her. This day, which was to be one of the happiest days of his life, has just fallen apart and he's exhausted emotionally. Armida said, she didn't care what her father said but he can't help but wonder if that's really true. He decides to stop at the church of Saint Pellico. This time it is to pray

CHAPTER 24

Carrying a fringed briefcase, Charlie Daytime enters Miguel's Albuquerque Gallery. He's dressed in a western-cut buckskin jacket decorated with beautiful Navajo pattern beadwork. As he glances around the gallery, his manner indicates that perhaps he still has a chip on his shoulder.

Miguel called Charlie after Armida informed him the second D.N.A. test has verified the blanket as Narbona's. Noticing Charlie's arrival from his desk on the mezzanine, Miguel hurries down and shakes Charlie's hand.

"Thank you for coming," he says. "This is important. I told you on the phone that I have something to show you. Please follow me."

Still looking somber, Charlie trails Miguel into the vault. "Have a seat," Miguel says, pointing to a stool. Miguel hands him a thick packet Armida has helped prepare, "Please look through this. It's the provenance."

Charlie studies the paperwork while Miguel dons white cotton gloves. In the packet is a Narbona bio, much the same as the same story told by Navajo elders to the young men of their family. Narbona is accurately portrayed as a powerful Navajo leader who had done everything in his power to settle with the Americans after the Mexicans gave up New Mexico and returned to Mexico. In 1864, he negotiated a treaty with the American commander at Bear Springs. The treaty was supposed to protect the Navajos from settlement and slave raids, also promising to open up trade with them. But sadly this treaty and the others which followed were doomed and by 1848 the Navajo nation was in complete disarray. Narbona was said to have been shot by the American governor Colonel James Marcre Washington in a dispute over a stolen horse.

Charlie's reading is interrupted when Miguel takes the old wearing blanket from the vault and carefully places it on the table. Removing the protective covering, he spreads the blanket out for inspection. "Here." he says, handing Charlie a pair of gloves. "Why don't you take a look at it?"

Without comment, Charlie goes over to the weaving, puts on the gloves and gently touches the bullet hole. His expressionless face gives little indication what he's thinking. "Why do you do this?" he asks. "Why do you show this to me?"

"I show you this because my intention is to donate the blanket to the Navajo Nation." Miguel answers. "I do this for the Dineh, not for Charlie Daytime. It rightfully belongs to your people, a sober page of their heritage. Narbona was a great man of peace. He was a brave leader, and his memory is one all Navajos should cherish. I have studied his life and understand why your people think so highly of him. His efforts to live up to the treaties he signed in good faith are well documented. Now, even the United States government admits they were less than honorable in their dealings with him and other Navajo leaders who acted in good faith. Some even admit the charges which brought about his death may have been trumped up."

Charlie looks up from the blanket. He's almost completely overwhelmed, yet he feels a strange mixture of pride and pleasure. He looks at Miguel with newfound appreciation. "Our people know of Narbona greatness."

"I must ask that you allow Doctor Valenzuela to display this blanket in her upcoming show on early Navajo textiles," Miguel continues, feeling good about himself for the first times since Carlos turned him down for Armida's hand in marriage. "I would also ask you give credit for the donation to a Mrs. Grace Well. I've got an appraisal letter for you to send her with a thank you note. With your help, she should also be able to get substantial tax break. Naturally, during the show, the museum will acknowledge the loan in your name and her's. Narbona's blanket will be on display for thirty days, then you can do with it what you wish."

Charlie still can't believe what's happening. Narbona was indeed one of the Navajo's most revered leaders, and his wearing blanket and its provenance will have great meaning to his people. He can't help but wonder if perhaps he has been wrong about this white man. He's certainly aware of the blanket's historic value and couldn't begin to estimate its cash value. Overcome with emotion, he stands there holding the blanket close to his chest. Looking directly at Miguel his eyes mist over and a single tear runs down his cheek. Then he carefully lays the blanket back on the table.

"I'm at a loss for words," he offers in a low voice. "This is a precious gift to my people. Of course the museum can display it. When word about what you have done is known, my people will come from all over our nation to visit it. I would like to take the blanket now and have Uaroba bless it. I will return it in one week. Is this satisfactory?"

"Of course," Miguel replies. "I have an agreement you need to sign and an invoice transferring ownership for the sum of one dollar. I would also ask you to send a letter to Mrs. Well, thanking her for the donation to your people."

Charlie reads the agreement, signs both copies and keeps one. From a little leather coin purse he removes an old silver dollar and hands it to Miguel, who in turn, gives him an envelope with Mrs. Well's home address written on it, an invoice marked paid by cash, and the provenance material.

"Will you see that Cora Begay gets this?" Miguel asks, handing Charlie another envelope with Cora's name on it. Inside is his check for two thousand dollars.

"Yes," Charlie assures him, smiling knowingly "I see her sister Desbah on a regular basis. I'll give it to her."

Miguel carefully re-wraps the old Narbona blanket, and places it in a carrying tube, then hands it to Charlie who places his right hand on Miguel's shoulder. "Senior Jaramillo, today you have done a great thing for my people. I thank you. My people thank you. May you always walk the rainbow way."

Then after shaking Miguel's hand, Charlie places all the materials in his briefcase and with the tube under his arm strides, head high, out of the gallery.

As he watches him leave, Miguel can't help but think that his father would have been proud.

CHAPTER 25

Armida is up early. It's been a week and she hasn't spoken to her father since she learned he refused to give permission for Miguel to marry her. His refusal has taken away all of the joy she experienced from the possibility of taking over the vineyard, and after another sleepless night, she's in a foul mood. She's already barked at her foreman and chewed out a crew working in the shed, when Carlos shows up in the lab.

"Good morning," Carlos offers. Armida simply looks away and continues making notes in a ledger. Carlos speaks again. "How goes the tally?"

Armida whirls around, her blue eyes flashing. "Papa, how could you turn down Miguel? I told you how I feel about him. Her voice begins to rise. What right have you to do such a thing?"

"I'm your father and I know what's best for you and the vineyard. You don't need to marry right now and especially not a Latino." His face is set and his look is a stern one.

Armida retaliates. "What do you think I am? A child? I'm thirty-nine years old and fully capable of making my own decisions." She's shouting now, tears streaming down her cheeks. "How could you do this to me?"

Carlos replies. "This is in your best interest and you better damn well understand that if you intend to take over the vineyard."

"So that's the way it is? Well you can just keep it all to yourself, if those are your terms. Go to hell!" She answers angrily. This is the first time she has ever cussed at her father, but she's out of control and throws the ledger at him. "I love Miguel." she screams and you can't stop me from becoming his wife. I've already told him I will marry him. Keep your damn vineyard." With that she storms out of the lab and twenty minutes later is packed and on her way to her condo in Albuquerque.

Two days later, she's on her way to Gran Quivira. She needs to get away. She's not spoken to her father since their blow up and she's still in a foul mood.

The trip takes her east on I-40 to Tijeras then south on N.M. Hwy. #337 through the little mountain community of Mountainair to N.M. Hwy. #55.

The scenery is spectacular as she travels along the eastern slopes of the Manzano Mountains through the Cibola National Forest southward to the Gallinas Mountain range. In Mountainair she stops at the new Salinas Pueblo Missions National Monument visitor's center. Gran Quivira National Monument is the southern most of the group of three contemporaneous pueblos consisting of Abo, Quarai and Gran Quivira. These mission sites are austere, yet beautiful reminders of the earliest contact between the Pueblo Indians and the Spanish Colonials. The juniper and pinon-covered slopes of the Chupadera Mesa rise to the west and southwest of Gran Quivira twenty-five miles south of

Mountainair. The mesa where the ruins are located is at a 6,600-foot altitude. Even now, Armida knows this hostile land remains virtually impossible to farm and the reason why the Jumano Pueblo Indians inhabited such a destitute area of New Mexico is still a mystery.

Twenty-five miles south of Mountainair, she winds her way through pinion and cedar-lined hills into the parking lot of the Gran Quivira Monument. A short distance down a dirt path, she comes upon a small, modern visitor's center. The Park Ranger, who is the custodian, is a nice looking young man who spends a half-hour with her discussing the ruins. Since he is about to close up and go to lunch he suggests she go ahead and walk the ruins and come back after he returns from lunch if she needs more information. Although she's curious where he is going for lunch in this lonely country, she says nothing.

Carrying the brochure he gave her, she leaves the museum and follows a well-marked dirt trail northward. She's gone about fifty yards when to her right she sees a gigantic blue gray limestone west wall of the San Isidro church, the largest excavated structure in the ruins, a dramatic presence, towering above her.

The dominating, reconstructed, thirty-foot limestone wall offers her first look at one of the seventeen pueblo ruins of Gran Quivira. The pueblo represents only a small part of the large Indian population that once occupied the general region on the east slopes of the Manzano range during the period of Spanish exploration and missionary activity.

Further along, the trail breaks sharply to the right and starts up a rather steep hill. Another hundred yards further along she finds herself on top of a small mesa. Here she encounters a soothing silence broken only by a constant breeze and the chirr of insect wings. Scarce desert flora and an occasional yucca plant partially hide the broken foundations of ancient stone houses built by Pueblo Indians who once inhabited the area. To her left are a series of excavated mounds revealed the remains of a large single story, multi-room apartment house and several ceremonial kivas, typical of Southwest Indian culture. Nearby, the ruins of two Spanish mission churches attest to the presence of Spanish priests in this desolate, isolated region. The quiet remnants of the village of Las Humanas now known as Gran Quivira only hint at the vibrant society, which once thrived here until the late seventeenth century.

The map given her by the custodian diagrams the existing walls and the, as yet, un-excavated seventeen mounds. For over an hour she wanders around through the sites. Finally, atop the highest wall of the San Isidro church ruins, she's able to get a perspective of the ruins and compare them to the photo of the design on the old weaving. Without question the remaining walls of the two church sites and three round kivas closely match the design on the weaving. Estimating the location of the spot indicated as the treasure site is the next challenge.

Referring to the photo, she stands on the wall and locates the indicated spot. Then climbs down and stands in a depression about 300 yards from the walls of the second church, the San Buenaventura. For a while she simply stands there with her thoughts of what might lay hidden below this depression. Then she goes back down the trail to the visitor center.

When she arrives at the museum, the young Ranger has returned from lunch. Armida gives him her card, and explains the purpose of her visit. He tells her he's aware of several attempts over the years to discover hidden gold at the site and verifies that the last permit for excavation was granted in 1933 and all the evidence of the 1933 excavation was back-filled in 1940 by the National Park Service. He goes on to suggest she get in touch with a retired park ranger who lives in Santa Fe. A man who is considered as the best-known expert on Gran Quivira. Then he warns her that her chances of getting a permit to excavate are very slim. Armida thanks him for his time and leaves for Albuquerque.

CHAPTER 26

Back at the Taylor museum, Armida prepares for her textile show. To her surprise, during the two weeks she has been trying to find out exactly what it takes to get a permit to excavate at the Gran Quivira site, the bureaucracy of the National Park Service so far has stonewalled her. Finally she realizes the only way she is ever going to obtain a permit is to have her father use his political clout, but for two days she has struggled with herself about calling him. Since their blowup, she has only seen him once when she went out to the rancho to pick up Mary and Jesse. She's not changed her mind about Miguel, and there's no indication her father has changed his. They are stalemated. Today, however, she decides to give him a call.

"*Hola*, Papa. How are you feeling?"

"*Hola*, Muchacha. Better. They've changed my medication."

"That's Great." Armida replies, noticing the stained tone in his voice. No doubt he's finding this conversation as difficulty as she is.

"Papa," she says. "Don't you know the man that's the Secretary of the Interior?"

"Juaro Martinez," Carlos answers. "Of course I do. He's a relative of ours. His mother was your grandmother's cousin. Why do you ask?"

"I'm trying to get a permit to take a look at the Gran Quivira site and see if the map on the old weaving I showed you is for real," Armida explains.

"I helped him get appointed," her father says. "He owes me. Do you want me to give him a call?"

Armida's heart fills with relief. " If you could. I'm not getting anywhere with those National Park Service people and they work for him, don't they?"

"That's right. I'll see what I can do." When are you coming up?" Carlos asks.

"I don't know. I'm swamped getting ready for the show and then we need to get to Gran Quivira," she replies.

"We need to talk, *Muchacha*." Carlos' voice quivers a little. "You should come up."

"Papa. I don't think we have anything to discuss. I'm trying to get on with my life and I've got a marriage to plan. Just make the call for me," she answers firmly.

"If that's the way you want it, I'll call Juaro today, te *amo Muchacha*."

"*Y yo te amo*, Papa."

Armida can't help but wonder if she and her father will ever patch up their differences. His rejection of Miguel hurt her deeply, and when he attempted to blackmail her by retracting his offer to turn over the vineyard, it was devastating. She knows her father to be a proud man but now she realizes he was also a selfish one. He wants things his way or else, making her consider the possibility that even if he had turned over running the vineyard to her, it would never really have been hers.

The next day the call comes. "My name is Bernice Ortega," the caller explains. "My boss, Juaro Martinez, asked me to call. It's our understanding you are having some kind of a problem with the National Park Service. Can I be of some assistance?"

For thirty minutes Armida explains what she needs and what the university's geology department has said it would require to accomplish the task. She indicates that if a permit which, would allow for core drilling and the sinking of a mineshaft were given, the University will supervise the work and restore any damage to the monument. She promises if the core and the use of some of the latest mineral detecting equipment indicates that something of significance is buried there, a shaft will be opened, and assures Bernice any materials found will be the property of the United States government.

"I'll see what I can do for you," Bernice tells her. "Juaro is out of the country, but please tell your father as soon as he returns, he will be in touch."

"Thank you so much. I'll be anxious to hear from you." Armida chuckles to herself. She can hear Carlos burning up the lines. He does love to exercise his political influence. She wants to thank him for his help, but decides it's not a good idea.

The next day a gentleman named Harold Ames from the district Office of the National Park Service in Santa Fe calls and asks her when she can come by and pick up her permit.

When Armida calls Miguel and tells him she will be in Santa Fe Saturday, he's delighted and asks her to stop by the gallery and have lunch.

Armida arrives at the Parks Service office right on time Saturday morning, bringing proof of insurance and a letter of bond commitment in case they are needed. Ames has his secretary there to handle the paper work. The processing goes smoothly, and as Armida suspected, they do need the insurance and bond information. Ames is very gracious and the permit gives the University 120 days to excavate, after they move onto the site

Ames thanks her for coming in and with the Gran Quivira permit in her purse, Armida drives to the Jaramillo gallery.

When Armida and Miguel finish a quiet lunch, they sit on a bench in a little park nearby. They have been there only a few moments when Armida decides to tell Miguel what has happened with her father. She held back her feelings during lunch, trying to remain calm, but now she looses it.

"Papa really doesn't want me to marry you. He tried to blackmail me by telling me if we marry, he will renege on his offer to let me take over the vineyard and winery." Armida is sobbing now, tears running down her cheeks. "I told him that he can keep the vineyard, but I've wanted to run them ever since I was little. I never dreamed he would not turn the operation over to me. I thought he loved me. Now I'm not sure. He loves his Castilian blood more than he loves me."

"What do you mean he loves his Castilian blood more than you?"

Miguel asks, taking her in his arms.

"It's the fact that you're a Latino," she replies. He's prejudiced against immigrants. He wants me to marry a Castilian man. It's apparently nothing against you personally, he just wants to keep our bloodline pure."

She pulls back and takes his face in both her hands.

"I love you Miguel and I told him that he can keep his damn vineyard." Once again she starts to cry.

"I've never loved any one as much as I love you," Miguel tells her. "But I don't want to come between you and your father, and I know how much the vineyard means to you."

Miguel has only recently begun to realize he has not always been fair to the Indians he traded with and now here he is taking away the dream of the woman he loves. How much damage can he do and still live with himself? He has the ring in his pocket and had planned to once again propose, but now he has doubts.

"Perhaps we should wait," he suggests. "I'm sure your father doesn't mean what he said."

Armida stares at him, shocked. Is Miguel backing out? Doesn't he want me as much as I want him? "Don't you want to marry me?" she blurts out, not trying to hide how much she's hurt. "No. No. Please don't misunderstand me," he begs. "I want to marry you. Today if you will have me. I just don't want to cause you any more trouble. Armida I love you."

Taking the ring from his pocket, he asks, "Will you marry me? Now today. We can fly to Las Vegas and be married before dark."

After placing the ring on her finger they kiss and Armida clings to him. "I want a real wedding, with all the trimmings," she says finally. "I want it to be perfect, and if Papa doesn't come, so be it. I truly do love you and want to be your wife."

Driving back to Miguel's gallery they make plans for the trip to Gran Quivira. "Have you located the special oilfield location equipment we will need for the core drilling?" Armida asks.

"Yes, I've been in touch with a guy who rents the equipment and his drilling rig is available."

"It's going to be a blast," Armida replies excitedly. "The folks from the geology department are ready to go and Ricardo is hot to trot. I've got the permits and the University has given us the green light. I can't believe our hunt for the fabulous 'Treasure of the Seven Cities of Gold' is about to begin.

CHAPTER 27

After three weeks of coordinating everything for the drilling and excavation project at Gran Quivira, they are ready to proceed. Armida stays in a University motor home she has parked in the visitor's center's parking lot, while Miguel has a room in Mountainair motel where the rest of the crew is staying. The University has been most generous to Armida, giving her their full cooperation for the project, and agreeing to underwrite the whole cost. Ricardo Flores, an oilfield mineralogist, and a geologist named Eric Adams have joined the group. To no one's surprise the first day's core samples fail to reveal anything unexpected. As the geologist predicted, the cores showed only limestone and some gypsum.

A newspaper reporter who got wind of the project because he's a friend of the owner of the core-drilling rig has written an article about the treasure hunt, which in turn has attracted two TV stations. Now their satellite TV vans are parked near the visitor's center and bored reporters are trying to get interviews with anyone who will speak to them. A small group of tourists and curious locals have gathered at the site, their presence has caused the forest service to restrict certain areas of the monument where the equipment is operating. Both Armida and Miguel have been interviewed for the evening news, which to their dismay is quickly assuming a circus-like atmosphere.

At the rancho, Carlos sees them together on TV. They are a great looking couple and in his heart he knows the only thing he really wants is Armida's happiness. He can't even think of his life without her in it. Miguel is not his choice but he is certainly Armida's and he knows that is all that really matters. It's time for him to accept this and make his amends. It's time he acknowledges their love. Standing there in front of the TV cameras it's obvious to him they make a great team.

He summons old Juan and tells him to get ready to drive him to Gran Quivira early the next morning. He needs to set things right. And now is the time to do so.

At the site, Armida stands by for the second day with Miguel and Ricardo. The early morning silence of the isolated site is once more broken by the rumble of the diesel engine powering a core drilling rig, while nearby the geologist and Miguel are discussing the project with the drilling foreman. The oilfield mineralogist who took a number of readings and has determined there is a sizable void in the ground below the area has suggested the location of the rig where Armida located the depression on her earlier trip. It's he who convinces Armida to order drilling to take place about twenty yards to the west, where he says he found unusual readings of something foreign.

Suddenly the geologist who has been examining a core sample says to

Armida. "I've only seen this type of deposit once in my life."

"What's so unusual about it?" she asks.

"It contains andersite, augite, feldspar, copper and what could be aluminum in volcanic ash and kaolin clay," he replies.

"What does that mean?" ventures a puzzled Miguel, who is standing next to Armida.

"It shouldn't be here, not in this area. The only place this combination was ever found is at the old Cerrillos Mine location on Turquoise Mountain south of Santa Fe."

"I don't understand what you mean," Armida prompts.

"This particular combination of minerals was once found in the overburden of the Cerrillos Turquoise mine," he told her. "For centuries the Cerrillos Mine yielded not only a unique form of turquoise but a history associated with many of the ancient native peoples of the Southwest. In fact, seventy-five colors have been identified ranging from tan to khaki-green to rich blue-green and the stone takes a brilliant polish. Pieces of Cerrillos turquoise have been unearthed in prehistoric ruins at the Pueblo Bonito in Chaco Canyon. So we know the Pueblo people used it as trade goods for centuries. It's entirely possible some of it came from here. At least there's certainly a possibility that what the Spanish hid here could be a turquoise mine site, not a gold site."

Everyone is stunned by what they hear. The first to speak is Miguel. "Let me get this straight. You're saying that we could be standing on the surface of a rich turquoise deposit?"

"That's exactly what I'm saying," the mineralogist confirms. "The Tiffany Company of New York alone extracted two million dollars' worth of high grade turquoise from the Cerrillos mine before it played out."

"When will we know for sure there is a turquoise deposit here?" asks the Park Service ranger.

"We need to pull some deeper samples and they should tell us," the geologist replies. "Go for it," Armida says.

Back in the University's motor home, Armida fixes Miguel and Ricardo a glass of iced tea and settles down to discuss what has happened.

"This is unreal," Miguel says. "A discovery of anything approaching the magnitude of the Cerrillos mine would be fantastic. When we were with the old Singer, he said, 'The long coats have taken our sky and hidden it from us.' That phrase has bothered me ever since he said it. But I guess I was so convinced we had a map for a hidden treasure of gold, I somehow dismissed what he had inferred."

"I should have picked up on it too," Armida adds. "Native Americans refer to turquoise as 'Sky Stone.' In their opinion it is far more valuable than gold. The Navajos refer to it as stone of the sky, stone of blessings, good fortune, protection, good health and long life."

Miguel nods in agreement. "A find of anything close to the Cerrillos deposit could be worth millions. And that old Singer knew it when he read the sign on that weaving."

Ricardo speaks up. "All these years we have been struggling to discover why Pueblo Indians would live in such a inhospitable place. If they did work a turquoise mine here, they would certainly have had good reason to put up with this godforsaken land. Turquoise could have been traded for anything they needed."

Their conversation is interrupted by Armida' cell phone. Answering it, she hears the voice of an excited geologist. "Doctor Valenzuela, we have turquoise."

They rush to the drill site and on the table lies a core with a bright blue streak. As a matter of fact, upon closer inspection, there appeared to be several veins of turquoise in the sample. Armida is stunned. So are the other members of their party. The first to speak is the geologist.

"It's the same as Cerrillos turquoise. I've seen enough samples now to guarantee it. My God! What a find!"

"All these years, treasure hunters have looked for gold and they were sitting right on top of a fortune in turquoise," Miguel says, "The famed Seven Cities of Gold stories should have included some mention of the color blue."

They had just returned to the mobile home when Juan drives into the parking with Carlos. Armida can't believe her eyes. Carlos gets out and heads straight for her. Taking her in his arms he says, "Muchacha, I'm so sorry. I was wrong. If you love this man I will not stand in your way.

I've been following your progress on the TV you two make a great team and I want to see you realize your dream. Can you ever forgive me?"

"Of course PaPa." She answers. "I love you and always have."

Realizing who Carlos and Armida are, one of the TV reporters covering the story of the find, films them standing there hugging each other and that night its broadcast on CNN National News. The whole world is now aware of the discovery and within minutes Armida receives a call from the University president asking for verification.

It takes several days of drilling, but they indeed determine they found a major turquoise deposit. At Armida's request, they drop a video camera into the void beneath the depression through a core hole, and the space turns out to be an underground passage that was probably where the Pueblo Indians mined and stored their turquoise, the true-Treasure of Gran Quivira.

In the months that follow, the National Park Service is faced with several problems, not the least of which is a suit filed by the Native American Indian Council to have the Gran Quivira turquoise deposit turned over to them. Soon after the story of the discovery was broadcast on CNN, Charlie Daytime filed a suit on the behalf of the Indians.

Epilogue

With Carlos' blessing Armida and Miguel are married in the beautiful church of Saint Dellico, and she's expecting a son in the spring. The Valenzuela wine from that year's vintage has been judged Gold Medal, and Armida Jaramillo is in the process of adding over one hundred acres of new varieties of Hybrid grapes to the vineyard.

The Dineh, children of the Spider woman, now have their sky back. The long coats have returned but they have not received the welcome once so freely given.

THE END